The Forged Coupon

Leo Tolstoy

Translated by Hugh Aplin

ET REMOTISSIMA PROPE

Hesperus Classics

Hesperus Classics

Published by Hesperus Press Limited

4 Rickett Street, London sw6 1ru

www.hesperuspress.com

First published in Russian in 1911

First published by Hesperus Press Limited, 2006

Introduction and English language translation © Hugh Aplin, 2006

Foreword © Andrew Miller, 2006

Designed and typeset by Fraser Muggeridge studio

Printed in Jordan by Jordan National Press

isbn: 1-84391-135-3

isbn13: 978-1-84391-135-7

CONTENTS

'I cannot drink flowers and chocolates', a sign above the detective's desk hinted to his visitors. Yes, the officer told me, as his colleagues fooled with their weapons: he could issue the certificate I needed, in order to replace the documents that had been stolen with my wallet in a Moscow restaurant. But there would have to be a 'stimulus' – to be precise, 500 roubles.

During my second year in Russia, a crime of haunting depravity allegedly occurred near the town of Samara. A small-time gangster wanted to hush up an informer. So the gangster kidnapped the informer, along with two randomly selected immigrant workers from central Asia. The gangster killed one of them and, to discredit him, forced the informer to kill the other.

In Nazran, southern Russia, lives a woman named Katya of whom you will not have heard. Katya is a saint. She comes from a good St Petersburg family, and once began a PhD in America. But she gave them up to live in Russia's wretched north Caucasus, where she documents the murders and kidnappings committed by the army and local paramilitaries. I last saw her in Grozny, skeletal capital of grim Chechnya, looking pale and thin. I was on a guarded, government-sponsored trip; Katya was not.

It can be convenient to see the pathologies of modern Russia as the legacy of Soviet rule – unless or until you read Tolstoy, whose characters and stories seem so often to be contending with the same problems Russians live with today. *The Forged Coupon* brilliantly conveys three that I have met. One is the regular failure of all state institutions – and, as Tolstoy saw it, of the Orthodox Church – whose representatives in this story, from the police up, are brutal, corrupt, capricious, vain and gluttonous (though Tolstoy also records the atavistic faith, which endures still, that the man at the very top 'alone felt pity for the common people and was just'). Another is the bizarre kind of ultra-violence that can happen in an atomised society, one in which even the memory of God has been forgotten. Those two, plus drink, drink, drink. But Tolstoy is a guide to the glories of Russian civilisation as well as its sicknesses, and here he dramatises the peculiarly Russian, otherworldly sort of goodness that, as in the north Caucasus today, has always lived alongside the badness.

The Forged Coupon is a crazily dexterous feat of storytelling. Its structure is as sophisticated and as simple as a fairy tale, as the batons of evil and then good are passed across Russia and back again. And as in *Hadji Murat* (another of Tolstoy's late, great novellas), he seems here to have set himself a sort of creative challenge: to squeeze all of Russia, from horse-thieves to the Tsar, town and country, Moscow to St Petersburg – everything, almost, that he put into *Anna Karenina* – into as few pages as possible. So we meet the inadvertently glamorous revolutionary; the phony churchman, most insulted by unbelievers when he knows the insults are true; the murderer who 'did it not as he had wanted'; the debutantes and politicians. We learn about the ruses used by nineteenth-century wood-sellers; see the English pigs on the farm; taste the pickled mushrooms and flavoured vodkas; graze the cold arm of the corpse in the mortuary.

All these fleeting meetings are drawn with that writerly quality that led some of Tolstoy's contemporaries to think he had been touched by divinity: a few strokes, and his characters spring from his pages whole, somehow familiar even if they work in a nineteenth-century photographic accessories shop. The panoramic sweep begins and ends with a perfect domestic vignette: the mutual incomprehension and submerged love of a father–son relationship. Mitya is angry and scared at the same time, as sons can be; his father Fyodor Mikhailovich is so moody that he doesn't even feel like eating, then immediately goes in to his dinner. Mitya resolves to become the villain that his irate dad (who will nevertheless do battle with his son's accusing teacher) says he is already. Spurned, Mitya turns to Makhin, a timeless portrait of bad influence, who 'played cards, knew women, and… always had money'. (Makhin, as bad influences must, goes on to law school, as indeed did Tolstoy himself, during the rakish youth that later agonised him.) There are concisely moving glimpses throughout of another sort of domestic rancour – the prison of unhappy marriage, and, especially, of what men do to women in them. There is the shopkeeper's wife, reminded by an argument of the death of her child, and alarmed by the strength of her own feelings; there is the freshly bereaved widow, with a sense of liberation that she must hide from herself.

In each little scene we find, in miniature, the complex histories and motives that make up every social interaction. But alongside them there is also a different sort of narrative and another kind of motive. In the middle of the story, Tolstoy the invisible narrator morphs into Tolstoy the preacher, and *The Forged Coupon* takes a theological turn that some readers will find disconcerting – though to me the striking thing is not that the religion interferes with the storytelling, but rather that the storyteller in Tolstoy is too mighty to be overwhelmed even here by the different preoccupations that competed with this instinct in the last decades of his life. (It is beautiful that, just before his conversion, the murderer remembers 'the benches he went sledding on with other children'.) This parallel narrative is about another kind of prison, the prison of the body and of sin, and about the idea of goodness that Tolstoy was developing: goodness not as active intervention in worldly affairs, but as non-resistance to evil, or 'absorption', as he called it in his diaries. Opposites though Dostoevsky and he were – claustrophobic though Dostoevsky is where Tolstoy is expansive, relentless where Tolstoy is compassionate – this dual approach reminds me somehow of *The Idiot*, which like *The Forged Coupon* is at once psychologically precise and a mystic parable.

But then part of the grandeur of the great Russian novelists is that they seem always to be stretching up their hands to heaven, grappling with the biggest questions, including that of the utility of art. By the time he wrote *The Forged Coupon*, Tolstoy had come to denounce the art that he nevertheless still practised. It is not his finest work, but it may be his most concentrated effort to reconcile his divergent ways of thinking and living. And at its heart is a question that would echo across Tolstoy's country for the rest of the century, after he died at his railway station in 1910: what might it mean to live in a world without God?

– Andrew Miller, 2006

INTRODUCTION

Work on *The Forged Coupon*, which was by Leo Tolstoy's established standards a brief work of fiction, extended over almost a quarter of a century of the author's later life, from 1880 to 1904. By comparison, the composition of each of his weightiest tomes, *War and Peace* and *Anna Karenina*, completed in six years in the 1860s and five years in the 1870s respectively, occupied decidedly short periods of time; the last of his long novels, *Resurrection*, written during the same period as *The Forged Coupon*, was completed in little more than a mere decade between 1889 and 1899. It was a general characteristic of Tolstoy's fictional writing that it was slower towards the end of his career, and there were a number of reasons why this was the case.

It is scarcely a shock, of course, if any author in his sixties is less prolific than he was when twenty years younger. Tolstoy's creative imagination, however, continued to flourish, and he consequently had any number of projects planned or in progress during, say, the 1890s, even though he regularly expressed his consciousness that he would never manage to bring them all to fruition. Thus several works would regularly be set aside to allow more rapid progress to be made on the text that had – even if only temporarily – the most pressing claims on the writer's attention. Even such an important short work as the late masterpiece *Hadji Murat* took eight years to complete, suffering a series of false starts and interruptions on the way – and without ever actually undergoing a final editing procedure. Moreover, at this late stage in his life Tolstoy's fictional writing had to vie for his energies with his voluminous work in other spheres, notably in that of religious writing. This non-fiction was what Tolstoy considered to be his more important contribution to Russian letters after the spiritual and aesthetic crises he underwent in the 1870s and 1880s, leading to his theoretical rejection of the novel. The logical consequence of this rejection – that is, the complete abandonment of creative writing – was, however, never fully realised, and the pull of his fictional projects was a force that he rarely managed to resist for long. He did, nonetheless, seek to alter the nature of his fiction in the closing decades of his life, to render it more appropriate, as he would have considered it, in the light of his artistic and ethical intentions. *The Forged Coupon* was certainly a text of which he could broadly approve.

The instructive purpose of *The Forged Coupon* is clear, and both the didactic aim and the clarity were important elements of Tolstoy's approach to creative literature after the completion of *Anna Karenina* in 1878. Paradoxically, the structure of the story is actually quite complex, as the interlocking lives and fates of a range of characters from different social backgrounds are traced out over a period of more than a decade. Yet within that structure the narrative is sparse and taut. Many of the features that had characterised the writer's great novels and other earlier works – extended dialogue, detailed description of settings, intense psychological analysis – are quite absent here, and all (or almost all – Vasily's escape from prison, for example, is a scene that takes on a little life of its own) serves to underline the book's major ethical and religious concerns. Equally, the dense, complex argumentation of the major philosophical stories of the 1880s, such as *The Death of Ivan Ilyich*, is avoided here. Tolstoy approaches in *The Forged Coupon* the simplicity of his tales for those learning to read, the popular short stories of the 1880s, and *A Prisoner in the Caucasus* – works that, however mistakenly, he ultimately deemed his only genuinely successful works of art.

The message of *The Forged Coupon* can be expressed quite simply – evil deeds beget further evil, while goodness breeds goodness. The apparently harmless schoolboy trick of falsifying the value of a coupon – these were detachable vouchers on government bonds that could be used for payment in lieu of banknotes – leads to a series of crimes in Part One of increasingly terrible consequence. The shorter Part Two, although not bereft of dark moments, illustrates how positive examples of a good Christian life and its characteristic virtues can throw light into any social setting, from the meanest to the most exalted. Just as the focus of *Hadji Murat* switches from the extremes of Caucasian villages to the Imperial court in St Petersburg, so does this work encompass life in both town and country, from the poorest peasant's hut to the dining-table of the Tsar, from the upper hierarchy of the Orthodox Church to the communal cell of a Russian jail. Here is the grand sweep of *War and Peace* in miniature, but with a much more clearly defined moral thrust – for the author now knows what is right. The villains are those who fail to recognise and live by the high standards of personal ethics that Tolstoy was himself trying to adopt from the 1870s onwards. Included in this category are the shopkeeper who seeks to recoup his losses at the expense of another man, the peasant who steals from his peers with no concern for the harm he causes, the man of God who pays lip-service to an institutionalised faith while having no genuine belief of his own, and the Tsar who exercises his rights as a ruler without recognition of his duties as a man. By contrast, the catalyst for the emergence of light is a humble and exploited woman who gives away her property and works for the benefit of others, never expecting a thing in return. Her family name is Dobrotvorov – 'doer of good' – and it is her example, passed on from person to person, that brings about a series of conversions that finally lead the reader back to the book's opening scene.

A key text within the story is that of the Sermon on the Mount. This passage from the Gospel According to St Matthew was also central to Tolstoy's *A Criticism of Dogmatic Theology* (1880), in which he set out his belief in the teachings' literal value as a blueprint for the conduct of life. A series of publications in the ensuing years further underlined his adoption of the Sermon's tenets, not only in his own personal life, but also as a guide to the way that, in his view, the nation's social life as a whole should be conducted. The roles of the secular authorities, of the educated ruling classes and of the Russian Orthodox Church in providing guidance on moral and religious issues all came to be called into question in his writings for their failure to observe the Sermon's requirements, and Tolstoy's critical stance towards the Church in particular finally led to his infamous excommunication in 1901. The open criticism of the Church in *The Forged Coupon* provides a fictionalised parallel to Tolstoy's real-life struggle with the Orthodox hierarchy in the years he was working on the story.

It is similarly characteristic of Tolstoy's world view in this period that the positive examples leading to redemption in the book stem fundamentally from the common people – even when mediation from members of other social strata is also involved. The Populist movement of the 1870s had put a great deal of faith in the positive qualities of the Russian peasantry, and even if much of the Populists' idealism had subsequently proved ill-founded, Tolstoy himself certainly believed there was a lot to learn from the way of life of the people. A number of his apparent eccentricities stemmed from his desire to adopt a lifestyle less in keeping with his privileged aristocratic birth, and more reminiscent of that of the common people with whom he liked to associate. Regularly chopping wood, wearing peasant-style dress, giving up rich food, doing without a servant and so on: all were intended to make his way of life more like that of a simple peasant, and thus more compatible with the teachings of Christ with respect to poverty and humility.

Just as Tolstoy had difficulty in living up to his own ideal of the Christian life, so the demands of art and the demands of didacticism led to a certain tension in fictions such as *The Forged Coupon*. Subtlety, for example, is certainly abandoned in favour of commitment. And, like other works that could only be published posthumously, the story would have benefited from a stringent final edit to iron out some apparent inconsistencies – indeed, the very rapid, perhaps excessive pace of the concluding chapters even suggests that a little more time might have been devoted to them beneficially. But this is still a work of remarkable vigour that sheds an interesting light on many of the concerns of Tolstoy's final decades, and virtually encapsulates his ultimate aesthetic and moral creeds.

– *Hugh Aplin, 2006*

The Forged Coupon

Part One

Fyodor Mikhailovich Smokovnikov, the President of the Provincial Revenue Department, a man of crystalline honesty and proud of it, a gloomy liberal, and not only a freethinker, but a hater of any manifestation of religious sentiment, something he considered a vestige of superstition, returned from the Department in the worst possible frame of mind. The Governor had sent him an extremely silly document, from which could be inferred the observation that Fyodor Mikhailovich had acted dishonestly. Fyodor Mikhailovich had grown angry and had there and then written a brisk and caustic reply.

At home it seemed to Fyodor Mikhailovich that everything was being done to defy him.

It was five minutes to five. He had thought that dinner would be served straight away, but dinner was not yet ready. Fyodor Mikhailovich slammed the door and went off to his room. Somebody knocked at the door. 'What the devil's this now?' he thought, and called, 'Who's that now?'

Into the room came a fifteen-year-old boy from class five of the grammar school, Fyodor Mikhailovich's son.

'What have you come for?'

'Today's the first of the month.'

'What? Money?'

It was the custom that on the first of each month the father would give his son an allowance for amusements of three roubles. Fyodor Mikhailovich frowned, got out his wallet, searched around and took out a coupon for two and a half roubles, then got out a purse with some silver in it and counted out another fifty kopeks. His son was silent and did not take it.

'Papa, can I have an advance, please?'

'What?'

'I wouldn't ask, but I borrowed against my word of honour, I promised. As an honest person, I can't… I need another three roubles, truly, I won't ask… well, it's not exactly that I won't ask, but simply… please, Papa.'

'You've been told…'

'Yes, Papa, but just this once…'

'You get an allowance of three roubles, and it's never enough. I didn't get even fifty kopeks at your age.'

'All my schoolmates get more now. Petrov and Ivanitsky get fifty roubles.'

'And I can tell you that if you're going to behave like this you're going to become a villain. Now I've told you.'

'So what if you have told me. You'll never put yourself in my position, I'll have to be a swine. It's all right for you.'

'Get out, you good-for-nothing. Out.'

Fyodor Mikhailovich leapt up and rushed towards his son.

'Out. You need a thrashing.'

The son took fright and grew angry, but grew angry more than he took fright, and, dropping his head, set off at a brisk pace towards the door. Fyodor Mikhailovich did not want to beat him, but he was glad of his rage, and shouted words of abuse for a long time yet, as he saw his son off.

When the maid came and said that all was ready for dinner, Fyodor Mikhailovich got up.

'At last,' he said. 'I don't even feel like eating any more.'

And knitting his brows, he went to have dinner.

At the table his wife started talking to him, but he growled out a curt reply so crossly that she fell silent. His son too kept his eyes on his plate and was silent. They ate in silence, and in silence they got up and went their separate ways.

After dinner the schoolboy returned to his room, took the coupon and the change out of his pocket and threw them onto the desk, and then took off his uniform coat and put on a jacket. First of all, the schoolboy took up a tattered Latin grammar, then he dropped the catch on the door, swept the money from the desk into a drawer with his hand, got some cigarette papers from the drawer, filled one, stopped it up with cotton wool, and started having a smoke.

He sat for a couple of hours with the grammar and his exercise books, taking nothing in, then got up and began walking about the room, stamping his heels, and recalling everything that had happened with his father. All his father's upbraiding words and, especially, his angry face came to mind as though he were hearing and seeing them right then. 'Good-for-nothing. Need a thrashing.' And the more he recalled, the more angry he got with his father. He remembered his father saying to him: 'I can see what you'll end up as – a villain. You mark my words.' – 'And you will end up as a villain too, if it comes to it. It's all right for him. He's forgotten the time when he was young. Well, and what crime is it I've committed? Simply went to the theatre, didn't have any money, borrowed off Petya Grushetsky. What's so bad about that? Anyone else would have felt sorry for me, asked about it, but that one only wants to have a go at me and think of himself. Now when it's him that hasn't got something or other, the shouting fills the whole house, whereas I'm a villain. No, he may be my father, but I don't love him. I don't know if everyone feels like that, but I don't love him.'

The maid knocked at the door. She had brought a note.

'They said to be sure to reply.'

In the note was written:

This is already the third time I've asked you to return the six roubles you borrowed from me, but you keep wriggling out of it. Honest people don't behave like this. Please send them immediately with this messenger. I need them badly myself. Surely it's not possible you can't get hold of them? Your friend, either contemptuous or respectful, depending on whether you return them or not,

– Grushetsky.

'Just think. What a swine. He can't wait. I'll have another try.'

Mitya went to his mother. This was his last hope. His mother was kind and did not know how to refuse, and she, perhaps, would indeed have helped him, but today she was anxious about the illness of her youngest, two-year-old Petya. She got cross with Mitya for coming and making a noise, and immediately refused him.

He muttered something under his breath and went out of the door. She felt sorry for her son and brought him back.

'Wait, Mitya,' she said. 'I haven't got it today, but I'll get hold of it tomorrow.'

But Mitya was still seething with anger towards his father.

'What good will it be tomorrow when I need it today? You'd better know, then, that I'll be going to see a friend.'

He went out, slamming the door.

'There's nothing else for it, he'll show me where to pawn my watch,' he thought, fingering the watch in his pocket.

Mitya got the coupon and change out of the desk drawer, put on his coat and set off to see Makhin.

2

Makhin was a schoolboy with a moustache. He played cards, knew women, and he always had money. He lived with his auntie. Mitya knew that Makhin was a bad boy, but when he was with him, he involuntarily deferred to him. Makhin was at home and getting ready to go to the theatre; his dirty little room smelt of perfumed soap and eau de cologne.

'This, my friend, is a rotten business,' said Makhin, when Mitya had recounted his woes to him, shown him the coupon and the fifty kopeks and said that he needed nine roubles. 'You can pawn your watch, yes, but you can do better too,' said Makhin with the wink of an eye.

'Better how?'

'Very simply.' Makhin took the coupon. 'Put a one in front of the two roubles fifty, and it'll be twelve roubles fifty.'

'But do such coupons actually exist?'

'But of course, and what about on thousand-rouble notes? I've passed one of them.'

'Have you really?'

'Well, shall I get on with it?' said Makhin, picking up his pen and smoothing out the coupon with a finger of his left hand.

'But it's wrong, isn't it.'

'Oh, what nonsense.'

'Absolutely right too,' thought Mitya, and again his father's abuse came to mind: 'A villain. And I will be a villain too.' He looked into Makhin's face. Makhin was looking at him, smiling calmly.

'Well then, shall I get on with it?'

'Go on.'

Makhin painstakingly traced out a one.

'Well, and now we'll go to a shop. Just here on the corner: photographic accessories. Quite opportunely, I do need a frame for this person here.'

He got out a photograph of a girl with big eyes, a huge hairdo and a magnificent bust.

'What a darling, eh?'

'Yes, yes. But how?…'

'Very simply. Let's go.'

Makhin put on his things and they went out together.

3

The bell rang in the entrance to the photographic shop. The schoolboys went in, looking around at the empty shop, its shelves stacked with accessories and with glass display cases in the counters. From the rear door there emerged a plain woman with a kind face and, going behind the counter, she asked what they wanted.

'A nice frame, Madame.'

'At what price?' asked the lady, quickly and deftly running her mittened hands with their swollen finger-joints over frames in various styles. 'These are at fifty kopeks, and these are a bit more expensive. And this is a very pretty new style, one rouble twenty.'

'Well, I'll have that one. But can't you give me a reduction? Take a rouble.'

'We don't allow haggling here,' said the lady with dignity.

'Well, good luck to you, then,' said Makhin, putting the coupon on the display case. 'Let's have the frame and the change, and quickly now. We mustn't be late for the theatre.'

'You've plenty of time,' said the lady, and began examining the coupon with myopic eyes.

'It'll be nice in this frame, eh?' said Makhin, turning to Mitya.

'Don't you have any other money?' said the shop assistant.

'That's just the problem, I don't. My father gave it to me, and I need to change it.'

'Surely you've got one rouble twenty?'

'I've got fifty kopeks. What is it then, afraid we're cheating you with forged money?'

'No, I didn't mean anything.'

'Give it back then. We'll get change.'

'So how much are you owed?'

'Well, it must be eleven roubles something.'

The shop assistant clicked away on her abacus, unlocked the desk, took out a ten-rouble note, and, moving her hand around in the small change, collected six twenty-kopek and two five-kopek coins as well.

'Be so kind as to wrap it up,' said Makhin, picking the money up unhurriedly.

'One moment.'

'The shop assistant wrapped it and tied it up with string.

Mitya drew breath only when the bell in the entrance rang behind them and they emerged into the street.

'Well, there's ten roubles for you, and you let me have this. I'll pay you back.'

And Makhin went off to the theatre, while Mitya went to see Grushetsky and settled up with him.

4

An hour after the schoolboys had left, the shop owner came home and began counting up the takings.

'Oh, you bungling idiot! What an idiot you are,' he shouted at his wife, seeing the coupon and immediately noticing the forgery. 'And why take coupons?'

'But I've been there when you've taken them yourself, Zhenya, specifically twelve-rouble ones,' said his wife, abashed, aggrieved and ready to cry. 'I don't know myself how they fooled me,' she said, 'those schoolboys. A good-looking young man, seemed so *comme il faut*.'

'*Comme il faut* idiot,' her husband continued scolding as he counted up the till. 'If I take a coupon, then I know and can see what's written on it. Whereas you, in your old age, appear to have just been having a good look at schoolkids' faces.'

His wife could not put up with that and got cross herself.

'A true man! Only capable of criticising others, but when you lose fifty-four roubles at cards yourself – that's all right.'

'I'm quite another matter.'

'I don't want to talk to you,' said his wife, went off to her room and began recalling how her family had not wanted to let her marry, considering her husband of much lower station, and how she alone had insisted on this marriage; she remembered about her child who had died and her husband's indifference to that loss, and she conceived such a hatred for her husband that she thought what a good thing it would be if he died. But upon thinking that, she took fright at her feelings and made haste to put her things on and go out. When her husband returned to the apartment, his wife was no longer there. Without waiting for him, she had put her things on and gone off alone to see a French teacher of their acquaintance who had invited them for the evening.

The French teacher, a Russian Pole, was serving high tea with sweet biscuits, and afterwards they sat down at several tables to play *vint*[1].

The photographic accessories' seller's wife sat down with the host, an officer, and a deaf old lady in a wig, the widow of a music shop proprietor, a great devotee and expert player. The photographic accessories' seller's wife had some luck with the cards. Twice she bid a slam. Beside her lay a plate with some grapes and a pear, and she was in cheerful spirits.

'Why's Yevgeny Mikhailovich not here yet?' asked the hostess from another table. 'We've got him down as our fifth player.'

'He's probably got engrossed in the accounts,' said Yevgeny Mikhailovich's wife, 'it's the payments for provisions and firewood today.'

And remembering the scene with her husband, she frowned, and her mittened hands began to tremble in anger towards him.

'Talk of the devil,' said the host, turning to Yevgeny Mikhailovich who was just coming in. 'Why so late?'

'Oh, various matters,' replied Yevgeny Mikhailovich in a cheerful voice, rubbing his hands. And, to his wife's surprise, he went up to her and said, 'You know what, I've passed that coupon.'

'Really?'

'Yes, to a peasant for firewood.'

And with great indignation Yevgeny Mikhailovich told everyone – and his wife inserted details into his account – how some unscrupulous schoolboys had duped his wife.

'Right, sir, now down to business,' he said, settling at the table when his turn came and shuffling the cards.

Yevgeny Mikhailovich had indeed passed the coupon to the peasant Ivan Mironov for firewood.

Ivan Mironov's trade was to buy one cubic *sazhen*[2] at the firewood stores, transport it around the town, and dole it out in such a way that the *sazhen* produced five quarters, which he sold at the same price as the cost of a quarter at the firewood yard. On this day, which was so unfortunate for Ivan Mironov, he had taken out an eighth early in the morning and, having quickly sold it, had loaded up another eighth, hoping to sell that, yet he had carried it around till evening, trying to get a customer, and no one had bought it. He kept coming upon experienced town-dwellers, who knew the usual tricks of peasants selling firewood and did not believe he had brought the firewood, as he assured them he had, from the country. He himself had grown hungry and frozen through in his worn sheepskin jacket and tattered peasant's coat; by evening the temperature had hit twenty degrees below zero; his old nag, which he did not spare, as he was intending to sell it to the knackers, had come to a complete standstill. So Ivan Mironov was prepared to sell the firewood, even at a loss, when he came upon Yevgeny Mikhailovich on his way home from going to the shop for tobacco.

'Take it, master, I'll let you have it cheap. The old nag's come to a complete standstill.'

'And where are you from?'

'We're from the country. Our own firewood, good and dry.'

'We know your sort. Well, what will you take?'

Ivan Mironov named a figure, began reducing it, and finally sold for the price he had wanted.

'Only for you, master, as it's not far to take it,' he said.

Yevgeny Mikhailovich did not haggle particularly, rejoicing in the thought that he would pass the coupon. Somehow or other, pulling on the shaft himself, Ivan Mironov brought the firewood into the yard and unloaded it himself into the shed. There was no yardman. At first Ivan Mironov was hesitant about taking the coupon, but Yevgeny Mikhailovich was so convincing and seemed such a lordly gentleman that he agreed to take it.

Going from the back porch into the maid's room, Ivan Mironov crossed himself, thawed out the icicles from his beard and, folding up the skirt of his kaftan, he took out his leather purse, and from it he took eight roubles fifty kopeks and gave back the change, while the coupon, after wrapping it in a piece of paper, he put into the purse.

Ivan Mironov thanked the master in the customary way and, no longer urging his old jade on with the knout, but with its handle – although the horse was scarcely capable of moving its legs, covered in hoar frost and doomed to die – he drove on, unladen, towards an inn.

Inside the inn, Ivan Mironov ordered himself eight-kopeks-worth of wine and tea and, having warmed up and even broken into a sweat, chatted in the most cheerful frame of mind with a yardman sitting at the same table as him. He became expansive with him and told him all his circumstances. Said he was from the village of Vasilyevskoye, twelve *versts*[3] from the town, that he was independent of his father and brothers and now lived with his wife and two children, the elder of whom merely went to college and did not yet help out in any way. Said he was staying in lodgings here and would go to the horse-market tomorrow, would sell his old nag and take a good look around, and if one took his fancy – he would buy a horse. Said he had now got together a rouble under twenty-five, and that half his

15

money was in a coupon. He got the coupon out and showed it to the yardman. The yardman was illiterate, but said he had changed such money for tenants, that it was good money, but some coupons were forged, and for that reason, to be on the safe side, he advised him to pay with it here at the bar. Ivan Mironov gave it to the waiter and asked him to bring his change, but the waiter did not bring the change, rather there appeared a bald bartender with a shiny face and with the coupon in his chubby hand.

'Your money won't do,' he said, indicating the coupon, but not giving it back.

'It's good money, a gentleman gave it me.'

'That's just it, that it's not good, but forged.'

'If it's forged, then give it here.'

'No, mate, your sort needs to be taught a lesson. You and some villains forged it.'

'Give me the money, what rights has you got?'

'Sidor! Call for a constable, will you,' the barman turned to the waiter.

Ivan Mironov was drunk. And when drunk he was troublesome. He seized the bartender by the collar and shouted:

'Give it back, I'll go and see the gentleman. I know where he is.'

The bartender pulled away from Ivan Mironov, and his shirt gave out a ripping sound.

'Ah, so that's the way you are. Hold on to him.'

The waiter seized Ivan Mironov, and at this point a constable appeared too. After listening, as a man in authority, to what was the matter, he immediately decided things.

'To the station.'

The constable put the coupon into his wallet and took Ivan Mironov, together with his horse, to the police station.

Ivan Mironov spent the night at the police station with drunks and thieves. It was already about midday when he was summoned to see the precinct police officer. The police officer questioned him and sent him with a constable to the seller of photographic accessories. Ivan Mironov had memorised the street and the building.

When the constable sent for the gentleman and presented him with the coupon and Ivan Mironov, who confirmed that it was this very gentleman that had given him the coupon, Yevgeny Mikhailovich put on a surprised, and then a stern face.

'Come, come, you've evidently taken leave of your senses. I've never seen him before.'

'That's a sin, master, and we're all going to die,' said Ivan Mironov.

'What's the matter with him? You've evidently been dreaming. You sold it to someone else,' said Yevgeny Mikhailovich. 'But still, wait, I'll go and ask my wife if she bought any firewood yesterday.'

Yevgeny Mikhailovich went out and immediately called the yardman, Vasily, a cheerful, good-looking, extraordinarily strong and agile young dandy, and told him that if he was asked where the most recent firewood had been bought, he should say it was at the stores, and that they did not buy firewood from peasants.

'Otherwise there's a peasant testifying that I gave him a forged coupon. The peasant's muddle-headed, saying God knows what, whereas you're a man with a level of understanding. Say just that, that we buy firewood only at the stores. And I've been meaning to give you this for a long time to buy a jacket,' added Yevgeny Mikhailovich, and gave the yardman five roubles.

Vasily took the money, flashed his eyes at the note, then at Yevgeny Mikhailovich's face, shook his hair and gave a faint smile.

'Of course, the masses are muddle-headed. Lack of education. Don't think of worrying. I know very well how to put it.'

No matter how much and how tearfully Ivan Mironov implored Yevgeny Mikhailovich to acknowledge his coupon, and the yardman to confirm his words, both Yevgeny Mikhailovich and the yardman insisted on their version: they had never bought any firewood from carts. And the constable took Ivan Mironov, accused of forging a coupon, back to the police station.

Only by following the advice of the drunken clerk who was sitting with him and giving the police officer a fiver did Ivan Mironov get out of his position under guard, without the coupon, and with seven roubles instead of the twenty-five he had had the day before. Ivan Mironov spent three of those seven roubles on drink, and went home to his wife dead drunk and with his face badly battered.

His wife was heavily pregnant and sick. She began scolding her husband, he pushed her away, she started hitting him. Without replying, he lay belly down on the plank-bed and burst into noisy tears.

Only the next morning did his wife realise what had been the matter, and, believing her husband, she spent a long time cursing the thieving gentleman who had tricked her Ivan. And Ivan, having sobered up, remembered the advice the workman he had been drinking with the day before had given him, and decided to go and complain to a barrister.

The barrister took the case on, not so much because of the money he could get, as because he believed Ivan and was indignant at how shamelessly the peasant had been tricked.

Both sides appeared at the trial, and the yardman Vasily was a witness. At the trial the same things were repeated. Ivan Mironov reminded them of God and the fact that we are going to die. Yevgeny Mikhailovich, although he was tormented by his consciousness of the vileness and danger of what he was doing, could not change his evidence now and continued to deny everything with an outwardly calm air.

The yardman Vasily received another ten roubles, and with a smile he calmly confirmed that he had never set eyes on Ivan Mironov. And when he was sworn in, although he was quailing inwardly, outwardly he calmly repeated the words of the oath after the old priest who had been summoned, swearing on the cross and the Holy Gospels that he would tell the whole truth.

The case ended with the judge rejecting Ivan Mironov's suit and deciding to exact from him legal costs of five roubles, which Yevgeny Mikhailovich magnanimously excused him. Letting Ivan Mironov go, the judge delivered him a lecture to the effect that he should be more careful in future in making accusations against respectable people, and should be grateful for the fact that he had been excused costs and was not being prosecuted for slander, for which he would have spent some three months in prison.

'We're humbly grateful,' said Ivan Mironov and, shaking his head and sighing, left the chamber.

It had all ended well, it seemed, for Yevgeny Mikhailovich and the yardman Vasily. But it only seemed so. Something happened that nobody saw, but that was more important than anything that people did see.

It was already more than two years since Vasily had left his village and started living in town. With every year he had been giving his father less and less money, and he had not sent for his wife, having no need of her. Here in town he had as many wives as you could want, and not like his modest peasant woman either. With every year, Vasily forgot village law more and more, and he felt at home with the ways of the town. There everything was coarse, grey, poor, disorderly, here everything was refined, good, clean, sumptuous, everything was in order. And he became more and more convinced that country folk lived without any level of understanding, like woodland beasts, while here there were proper people. He read books by good authors, novels, went to performances at the People's House[4]. In the village you don't see that sort of thing even in your dreams. In the village the old people say: live lawfully with your wife, toil, don't eat more than necessary, don't show off, but here people are clever, learned, so they know the true laws, and they live for their own pleasure. And everything is good. Until the business with the coupon, Vasily had never believed that gentlemen had no law whatsoever about how to live. It had always seemed to him that he did not know their law, yet a law there was. But after the business with the coupon and, most importantly, his false oath, of which, despite his terror, nothing bad came, rather, on the contrary, another ten roubles came, he was utterly convinced that there are no laws and one must live for one's own pleasure. Thus he had been living, and thus he continued to live. At first he only made himself a profit on shopping he did for the tenants, but that was insufficient for all his expenses, and, where he could, he started pinching money and valuables from tenants' flats, and he stole Yevgeny Mikhailovich's purse. Yevgeny Mikhailovich established his guilt, yet did not bother going to court, but rather dismissed him.

Vasily did not fancy going home, and he stayed on living in Moscow with his lady friend, looking for a job. A poorly paid job turned up as yardman to a shopkeeper. Vasily took it, but the very next month he was caught stealing sacks. The owner did not bother making a complaint, but gave Vasily a beating and fired him. After this incident, work was no longer to be found, but their money was being spent, and then clothing began to be sold and the proceeds spent, and it ended up with just one ripped jacket, a pair of trousers and down-at-heel shoes remaining. His lady friend got rid of him. But Vasily had not lost his bright and cheerful disposition and, after waiting until the spring, he set off on foot for home.

9

Pyotr Nikolayevich Sventitsky, a thickset little man in dark glasses (he had problems with his eyes and was threatened with total blindness), got up as usual before first light and, after drinking a glass of tea, put on a cloth-covered sheepskin coat trimmed with lambskin and set off around his farm.

Pyotr Nikolayich had been a customs official and had acquired eighteen thousand roubles in the service. He had retired some twelve years before, not entirely of his own free will, and bought the small estate of a young landowner who had squandered his entire fortune. Pyotr Nikolayich had been married while still working. His wife was a poor orphan from an old noble family, a large, plump, good-looking woman who did not give him any children. Pyotr Nikolayich was a thorough and persistent man in all his dealings. Knowing nothing about farming (he was the son of a member of the Polish gentry), he took farming up so successfully that in ten years the bankrupted eight-hundred-acre estate had become a model farm. All his buildings, from the house to the barn and the covering over the fire-hose, were solid, sound, roofed in iron and punctually painted. In orderly fashion in the implement-shed there stood carts, wooden ploughs, ploughshares, harrows. The harness was oiled. The horses, almost all from the farm's own stud, were not large, were light-brown in colour with black manes and tails, were well-fed, strong, and all looked alike. The threshing-machine worked in a roofed threshing-barn, the fodder was gathered in a special shed, the fertilising swill drained into a paved pit. The cows, also bred on the farm, were not large, but were high-yielding. The pigs were English. There was a poultry-yard with hens of a particularly good laying breed. The trees in the fruit orchard had a protective wash and additional planting went on. Everywhere everything was well-managed, solid, clean, in good order. Pyotr Nikolayich rejoiced in his farm and was proud of the fact that he achieved all this not by oppression of the peasants, but on the contrary, by strict fairness to them. Even when amongst the gentry he adhered to a middling, liberal rather than conservative view, and always defended the common people before advocates of serfdom. Be good to them, and they will be good. True, he did not let the blunders and mistakes of workmen pass, sometimes he even pushed them about a bit himself and demanded work, but on the other hand accommodation and grub were the very best, wages were always paid on time, and on holidays he treated everyone to vodka.

Stepping cautiously over the thawing snow – it was in February – Pyotr Nikolayich went past the draught-horse stable in the direction of the hut where the workmen lived. It was still dark, darker still because of a mist, but in the windows of the workmen's hut light could be seen. The workmen were getting up. He intended hurrying them: their orders were to take the six-in-hand and go to the copse for the last of the firewood.

'What's this?' he thought, seeing the stable door open.

'Hey, who's there?'

No one answered. Pyotr Nikolayich went inside the stable.

'Hey, who's there?'

No one answered. It was dark, soft underfoot, and it smelt of manure. In the stall to the right of the door lived a pair of young, light-brown horses. Pyotr Nikolayich reached out a hand – empty. He felt with a foot. Perhaps they'd lain down? His foot met with nothing. 'Where on earth have they taken them out to?' he thought. They weren't being harnessed, the sleighs were all still outside. Pyotr Nikolayich went out of the door and shouted loudly:

'Hey, Stepan!'

Stepan was the senior workman. He was just then coming out of the workmen's hut.

'Yeah!' Stepan responded cheerily. 'Is that you, Pyotr Nikolayich? The lads are just on their way.'

'What's the stable doing unlocked?'

'The stable? I can't say. Hey, Proshka, give us a lantern.'

Proshka ran up with a lantern. They went into the stable. Stepan understood immediately.

'It was thieves, Pyotr Nikolayich. The padlock's been knocked off.'

'Are you kidding?'

'They've taken them, the scoundrels. Mashka's gone. Hawk's gone. No, Hawk's here. Dapple's gone. Beauty's gone.'

Three horses were missing. Pyotr Nikolayich said nothing.

He frowned, and his breathing was heavy.

'Oh, if I could get my hands on him. Who was on watch?'

'Petka. Petka slept through it.'

Pyotr Nikolayich lodged a complaint with the police, the district police officer, the Land Captain, sent his own men out. The horses were not to be found.

'The filthy peasants!' said Pyotr Nikolayich. 'Look what they've done. Haven't I been good to them? Just you wait. Scoundrels, all scoundrels. I'll be doing things differently with you now.'

10

But the horses, the three light-browns, were already far away. One, Mashka, had been sold to gypsies for eighteen roubles, the second, Dapple, had been traded with a peasant more than forty *versts* away, Beauty had been ridden too hard and put down. The coat was sold for three roubles. The organiser of this entire business was Ivan Mironov. He had worked for Pyotr Nikolayich and knew Pyotr Nikolayich's ways, and he had decided to get his money back. And he had arranged the thing.

After his misfortune with the forged coupon Ivan Mironov drank for a long time, and everything would have gone on drink if his wife had not hidden from him the horse's collars, their clothing and everything else that could go on drink. During his drinking bout Ivan Mironov thought incessantly, not only about the man who had wronged him, but also about all the gentlemen and fine little gents who lived only by robbing the likes of him. On one occasion Ivan Mironov was drinking with some peasants from the vicinity of Podolsk. And the peasants, while walking along, drunk, told him about how they had stolen the horses away from another peasant. Ivan Mironov started criticising the horse-thieves for having done damage to a peasant. 'It's a sin,' he said, 'a horse is just the same as a brother for a peasant, and you go and deprive him of it. If they're to be taken, then it should be from the masters. Those dogs deserve it.' The further they went, the more they warmed to their theme, and the Podolsk peasants said that getting away with gentlemen's horses was not so easy. You needed to know all their movements, and without a man on the inside it was impossible. Then Ivan Mironov remembered about Sventitsky, with whom he had stayed as a workman, remembered that, when settling up, Sventitsky had docked him a rouble and a half for a broken kingpin, and also remembered the nice light-brown horses he had worked with.

Ivan Mironov went to see Sventitsky as if to get work, but with the sole purpose of spying and finding everything out. And having found everything out, that there was no one on guard and the horses were in loose boxes in the stables, he led the thieves there and did the whole thing.

After sharing the proceeds with the Podolsk peasants, Ivan Mironov arrived home with five roubles. At home there was nothing for him to do: he had no horse. And from that time on Ivan Mironov began associating with horse-thieves and gypsies.

11

Pyotr Nikolayich Sventitsky tried with all his might to find the thief. Without a man on the inside the thing could not have been done. And for that reason he started suspecting his own people and, having learned from enquiries of the workmen who had not spent that night at home, he found out that Proshka Nikolayev had not done so – a young fellow who had just arrived after doing military service in the army, a handsome, bright fellow whom Pyotr Nikolayich took as a coachman when going out. The district police officer was a friend of Pyotr Nikolayich's, he knew the district Chief of Police and the Marshal of the Nobility, the Land Captain and the investigator. All these persons were at his house on his name-day and knew his tasty fruit-flavoured vodkas and his pickled mushrooms – boletuses, honey- and milk-agarics. Everyone felt sorry for him and tried to help him.

'There, and you defend the peasants,' said the district police officer. 'It was the truth when I said they were worse than wild animals. Without a knout and a rod you can't do a thing with them. So you're saying Proshka, the one that drives around with you as your coachman?'

'Yes, him.'

'Let's have him in here.'

They summoned Proshka and started questioning him.

'Where were you?'

Proshka shook his hair, his eyes gleamed.

'At home.'

'What do you mean, at home, all the workmen testify you weren't there.'

'As you wish.'

'It's got nothing to do with what I wish. So where were you?'

'At home.'

'Well, all right then. Officer, take him away to the station.'

'As you wish.'

Proshka never did say where he was, and he did not say because he had spent the night with his lover, with Parasha, and he had promised not to give her away, and give her away he did not. There was no evidence. And Proshka was released. But Pyotr Nikolayich was certain it was all Prokofy's doing, and he started to hate him. One time, having taken Prokofy as his coachman, Pyotr Nikolayich sent him out to see to the relay horses. Proshka, as he always did, bought two measures of oats at the coaching inn. He fed a measure and a half to the horses, and had a drink on half a measure. Pyotr Nikolayich learned of this and took it to the Justice of the Peace. The Justice of the Peace sentenced Proshka to three months in jail. Prokofy had high self-esteem. He considered himself superior to people and was proud of himself. Jail humbled him. He could not feel proud in front of everyone, and he immediately became despondent.

Proshka returned home from jail embittered, not so much towards Pyotr Nikolayich as towards the whole world.

As everybody said, after jail Prokofy went to pieces, became too lazy to work, started drinking, and was soon caught stealing clothes from a tradeswoman and ended up in jail again.

And the only thing Pyotr Nikolayich learned about the horses was that the coat of a light-brown gelding was found, which Pyotr Nikolayich identified as Beauty's coat. And this, the thieves' impunity, irritated Pyotr Nikolayich still more. He could not now see any peasants, nor speak of them without malice, and where he could he tried to keep them down.

12

Despite the fact that, having passed the coupon, Yevgeny Mikhailovich stopped thinking about it, his wife, Maria Vasilyevna, could forgive neither herself for falling for the deceit, nor her husband for the cruel words he had used to her, nor, most importantly, those two good-for-nothing boys who had deceived her so cleverly.

From that very day when she had been deceived she scrutinised all grammar-school pupils carefully. Once she did encounter Makhin, but she failed to recognise him because, upon seeing her, he pulled such a face that it completely altered his looks. But Mitya Smokovnikov, when coming upon him face to face on the pavement a couple of weeks after the event, she did recognise immediately. She let him pass, and, turning back, followed after him. Having gone all the way to his apartment and found out whose son he was, she went the next day to the grammar school, and in the entrance hall encountered the Divinity teacher, Mikhail Vvedensky. He asked what she wanted. She said she wished to see the Headmaster.

'The Headmaster isn't here, he's unwell; perhaps I can do something or give him a message?'

Maria Vasilyevna decided to tell the Divinity teacher everything.

Vvedensky, the Divinity teacher, was a widower, a former Ecclesiastical Academy student and a very vain man. He had already encountered Smokovnikov's father in a certain gathering the previous year and, clashing with him in a conversation about faith, during which Smokovnikov had defeated him on every point and made him a laughing stock, he had decided to pay particular attention to the son, and, finding in him the same indifference to Divinity as in his unbelieving father, he had begun victimising him, and had even failed him in his examination.

On learning from Maria Vasilyevna of the young Smokovnikov's deed, Vvedensky could not help but feel pleasure, finding in this incident confirmation of his assumptions about the immorality of those who lacked the guidance of the Church,

28

and he decided to exploit this incident, as he tried to convince himself, as evidence of the danger that threatens all those who defect from the Church – but in the depths of his heart, as a means of revenge against a proud and self-confident atheist.

'Yes, very sad, very sad,' said Father Mikhail Vvedensky, his hand stroking the smooth sides of his pectoral cross. 'I'm very glad that you've handed the matter over to me; as a minister of the Church, I shall try not to leave the young man without instruction, but I shall try to soften the edification as much as possible.'

'Yes, I shall do as befits my calling,' Father Mikhail said to himself, thinking that, having completely forgotten the father's ill-will towards him, he had only the good and salvation of the youth in mind.

In the Divinity lesson the next day Father Mikhail related the entire episode of the forged coupon to the pupils and said it had been done by a grammar-school boy.

'A bad, a shameful deed,' he said, 'but denial is even worse. If, as I do not believe, it was one of you that did it, then it is better for him to repent than to hide himself.'

As he was saying this, Father Mikhail stared at Mitya Smokovnikov. The schoolboys, following his gaze, looked around at Smokovnikov too. Mitya blushed, sweated, then finally burst into tears and ran out of the class.

Mitya's mother, on learning of this, extracted the whole truth from her son and rushed to the photographic accessories shop. She paid the mistress twelve roubles fifty kopeks and persuaded her to conceal the schoolboy's name. And she ordered her son to deny everything and on no account to confess to his father.

And indeed, when Fyodor Mikhailovich found out what had happened at the grammar school, and his son, having been summoned, said no to everything, he went to see the

Headmaster and, after recounting the whole business to him, said that the Divinity teacher's action had been reprehensible in the highest degree, and he was not just going to let it drop. The Headmaster called for the priest, and a heated discussion took place between him and Fyodor Mikhailovich.

'A stupid woman mistakenly identified my son, then disavowed her testimony herself, and you could find nothing better to do than slander an honest, truthful boy.'

'I wasn't slandering him, and I won't allow you to speak to me like that. You're forgetting my office.'

'I don't give a damn for your office.'

'Your false notions,' began the Divinity teacher, his chin trembling so that his wispy little beard shook, 'are well known to the whole town.'

'Gentlemen, Father,' the Headmaster tried to calm the arguing men. But it was impossible to calm them.

'It's a duty of my office for me to concern myself with religious and moral education.'

'Enough of this pretence. As if I don't know you don't believe in either heaven or hell.'

'I consider it beneath my dignity to speak with a gentleman such as you,' said Father Mikhail, insulted by Smokovnikov's last words, particularly because he knew they were true. He had gone through an entire course at the Ecclesiastical Academy, and for that reason he had not believed in what he professed and preached for a long time now, but believed only that everybody should force themselves to believe in what he forced himself to believe in.

Smokovnikov was not so much indignant at the Divinity teacher's action, as of the opinion that this was a good illustration of the clerical influence beginning to manifest itself in Russia, and he told everyone about the incident.

And Father Vvedensky, seeing manifestations of firmly established nihilism and atheism not only in the young, but in
the older generation, became more and more convinced of
the necessity to struggle with it. The more he condemned the
unbelief of Smokovnikov and those of his ilk, the more he
became convinced of the firmness and stability of his own faith,
and the less he felt any requirement to test it or to reconcile it
with his life. His faith, recognised by the whole of the world
around him, was for him the main weapon in the struggle against
those who denied it.

These thoughts, provoked in him by the clash with Smokovnikov, together with troubles at the grammar school resulting
from that clash – namely, a dressing down and a reprimand from
the authorities – compelled him to take a decision that had
already been attracting him for a long time, since the death of his
wife: to embrace monasticism and elect for the very career path
down which some of his fellows from the Academy had gone,
one of whom was already an archbishop, another an archimandrite in line for a bishopric.

Towards the end of the academic year Vvedensky abandoned the grammar school, took monastic vows under the
name of Misail, and very soon obtained a post as rector of a
seminary in a town on the Volga.

1 3

Meanwhile, Vasily the yardman was taking the highway to the
south.

He walked through the day, and for the night a peasant
policeman would take him away to his next lodging. Everywhere
he was given bread, and sometimes he was even sat down at the

table to eat supper. In one village where he spent the night in the Orel Province he was told that a merchant who had rented an orchard from a landowner was looking for likely young watchmen. Vasily was sick of begging, but he did not fancy going home, and he went to the merchant with the orchard and got a job as a watchman for five roubles a month.

Life in a hut of straw and twigs was very pleasant for Vasily, especially after the apple trees began to ripen and the watchmen brought from the master's threshing-floor huge great trusses of fresh straw straight from under the threshing-machine. Lie the whole day long on fresh, aromatic straw beside piles of early- and late-cropping apple windfalls, even more aromatic than the straw, keep an eye on whether any kids have got in after the apples anywhere, whistle to yourself and sing songs. And Vasily was an expert singer of songs. And he had a good voice. Peasant women and girls would come from the village for apples. Vasily would have a joke with them, would give them more or fewer apples, depending on how much they took his fancy, in return for eggs or kopeks – and lie there again; he only had to get up to have breakfast, dinner and supper.

Vasily wore the one pink cotton shirt, and that was full of holes, he had nothing on his feet, but his body was strong and healthy, and when the porridge pot was taken off the fire, Vasily would eat enough for three, so that the old watchman simply wondered at him. At night Vasily did not sleep, and either whistled or gave a shout every so often, and, like a cat, he saw a long way in the dark. Once, some big lads from the village got in to shake down some apples. Vasily crept up and went for them; they tried to beat him off, but he sent them all flying, and one of them he took back to his hut and handed him in to the owner.

Vasily's first hut was in the far orchard, but the second hut, when those apple trees had finished, was forty paces from the master's house. And Vasily had even more fun in this hut. The whole day Vasily could see the master and mistress and the young ladies playing, going out riding, going for walks, and in the evening and at night playing the fortepiano, the violin, singing, dancing. He could see the young ladies sitting on the window sills with students and exchanging caresses, and then going out strolling by themselves in the dark lime-tree walks, where only strips and splashes of moonlight penetrated. He could see the servants running around with food and drink, and how the cooks, laundresses, stewards, gardeners, coachmen – all worked only to provide food and drink and entertainment for the masters. Sometimes the young masters dropped in on him in his hut, and he would select for them and hand them the best, juicy, rosy-cheeked apples, and the young ladies would bite into them straight away, their teeth crunching, and praise them, and say something – Vasily understood it to be about him – in French, and make him sing.

And Vasily feasted his eyes on this life, remembering his life in Moscow, and the idea that it was all a matter of money lodged itself more and more firmly in his head.

And Vasily began to think more and more about how things could be done so as to get hold of a good lot of money in one go. He started to recall how he had profited previously, and decided he needed not to do it like that, that he needed not to grab what was left lying around, as previously, but to think things out in advance, find everything out and do it cleanly, so as to leave no loose ends. By the Nativity of the Mother of God[5] the last late-cropping apple had been picked. The master made a good profit and, when settling up, showed his gratitude to all the watchmen, including Vasily.

Vasily dressed himself – a young gentleman had presented him with a jacket and a hat – and did not go home, for it made him feel really sick, thinking about the coarse life of the peasant, but went back into town with the hard-drinking soldiers who had kept watch on the orchard with him. In town that night he decided to break into and rob the shop whose owner, when he had stayed with him, had given him a beating and fired him without payment. He knew all the ins and outs and where the money was, he set a soldier to keep watch, and he himself forced a window from the yard, climbed through and took all the money. The job was done expertly, and no traces whatsoever were found. The money he took was 370 roubles. A hundred roubles Vasily gave to his companion, and with the remainder he left for another town, and there he hit the bottle with companions both male and female.

14

In the meantime, Ivan Mironov had become a skilful, bold and successful horse-thief. Afimya, his wife, who had scolded him previously for bad business, as she used to say, was now content and proud of her husband, of the fact that he had a cloth-covered sheepskin coat, and she herself had a shawl and a new fur coat.

In the village and in the surrounding district everyone knew that not a single theft of horses could be managed without him, but people were frightened of informing on him, and even when he was under suspicion, he came out clean and innocent. His latest theft was from the night pasture at Kolotovka. When he could be, Ivan Mironov was choosy about who he stole from, and best of all he liked taking from landowners and merchants. But it was also more difficult from landowners and merchants. And so, when landowners' and merchants' horses were unsuitable, he took from peasants too. And thus from the night pasture at Kolotovka he had seized whatever horses came to hand. The job was done not by him himself, but by a smart fellow he had put up to it, Gerasim. The peasants missed their horses only at dawn and rushed off to look for them along the roads. But the horses were standing in a gully in a state-owned wood. Ivan Mironov intended keeping them there until the next night, and then driving them forty *versts* in the night to a yardman he knew. Ivan Mironov paid Gerasim a visit in the wood, brought him some pie and vodka, and set off for home by a woodland path where he hoped to meet no one. Unfortunately for him, he bumped into a soldier on guard.

'Been out looking for mushrooms, have you?'

'There aren't any today,' replied Ivan Mironov, indicating the basket he had taken just in case.

'No, it's not the summer for mushrooms at the moment,' said the soldier, 'perhaps there'll be some later,' and he went on by.

The soldier realised there was something wrong here. There was no reason for Ivan Mironov to be walking through a state-owned wood early in the morning. The soldier returned and began a sweep through the wood. By the gully he heard the snorting of horses and went quietly to the spot from where he heard it coming. The vegetation in the gully was trodden down and there were horse droppings. Further along sat Gerasim, eating something, and two horses stood tethered by a tree.

The soldier ran to the village, took the village elder, the village policeman and two witnesses. From three sides they approached the spot where Gerasim was and seized him.

Gerasim did not bother denying anything, and in his cups immediately confessed to everything. He told how Ivan Mironov had plied him with drink and put him up to it, and how he had promised to come to the wood for the horses that day. The peasants left Gerasim and the horses in the wood, and they themselves set up an ambush, waiting for Ivan Mironov. When it had got dark, a whistle rang out. Gerasim responded. No sooner had Ivan Mironov begun to descend the slope than he was fallen upon and taken to the village. In the morning a crowd gathered in front of the village elder's cottage.

They brought Ivan Mironov out and began questioning him. Stepan Pelageyushkin, a tall, rather stooped, long-armed peasant with an aquiline nose and a sombre expression, began questioning him first. Stepan was an independent man who had done military service. No sooner had he left his father and begun to get by, than his horse had been stolen. After working for a year in the mines, Stepan had again procured two horses. Both had been stolen.

'Talk, where are my horses,' began Stepan, turning pale with anger, gazing sombrely now at the ground, now into Ivan's face.

Ivan Mironov denied all knowledge. Then Stepan struck him in the face and broke his nose, from which the blood began to run.

'Talk, or I'll kill you!'

Ivan Mironov, his head bent, was silent. With his long arm Stepan struck him once, twice. Ivan was still silent, only tossing his head first one way, then the other.

'Everybody hit him!' shouted the village elder.

And everybody started hitting him. Ivan Mironov fell down silently then shouted, 'Barbarians, devils, beat me to death. I'm not scared of you!'

Then Stepan grabbed a stone from a large pile of them that had been made ready, and split Ivan Mironov's head open.

15

Ivan Mironov's murderers were put on trial. Among those murderers was Stepan Pelageyushkin. The accusations against him were more serious than against the others because everybody testified that he had split Ivan Mironov's head open with a stone. Stepan concealed nothing in court, explained that, when his latest pair of horses had been stolen, he had made a statement at the district police station, and the trail could have been found by following the gypsies, but the district superintendent of police had not even let him into his sight and had made no search whatsoever.

'What are we to do with someone like that? He ruined us.'

'And why did others not hit him, while you did?' said the prosecutor.

'That's not true, everybody hit him, the village council had settled on killing him. And I only finished him off. Why torment him needlessly?'

The judges were struck by the expression of total composure with which Stepan told of his action, and of how Ivan Mironov had been beaten and he had finished him off.

Stepan really did see nothing terrible in this murder. In the army he had been obliged to execute a soldier by shooting, and just as then, so at the murder of Ivan Mironov, he saw nothing terrible. He had been killed – so be it. Today him, tomorrow me.

Stepan was given a light sentence, a year in prison. His peasant's clothing was taken off him and put into store under a number, and he had a prisoner's overall and slippers put on him.

Stepan had never had any respect for the authorities, but now he was utterly convinced that all the authorities, all the masters, all except the Tsar, who alone felt pity for the common people and was just, all were scoundrels, sucking the blood from the common people. The accounts of the exiles and convicts he became friends with in prison confirmed such a view. One was being sent to do hard labour in exile for having exposed the authorities' thieving, another for having struck a superior when he started distraining peasants' property for no good reason, a third for having forged assignats. Masters, merchants, no matter what they did, they got away with everything, while the poor peasant was sent to jail to feed the lice for each and every thing.

His wife visited him in jail. Things had been hard enough for her without him as it was, and then she had been burnt out as well and completely ruined, and she and the children had started begging. His wife's calamities embittered Stepan still more. In jail he was bad-tempered with everyone too, and once almost killed a cook with an axe, for which he was given an extra year. In that year he learned that his wife had died and that he no longer had a home...

When Stepan's term was up, he was called to the stores, the clothing he had arrived in was taken from the shelf and given to him.

'And where shall I go now?' he said to the quartermaster-sergeant while getting dressed.

'Home, of course.'

'I don't have a home. I probably ought to go on the road. Robbing people.'

'Go robbing, and you'll end up with us again.'

'Well, that's as may be.'

And Stepan left. He went in a homeward direction after all. There was nowhere else for him to go.

Before he reached home, he dropped in to a coaching inn that he knew to spend the night.

The inn was kept by a fat tradesman from the town of Vladimir. He knew Stepan. And he knew he had landed in jail by misfortune. And he let Stepan spend the night there.

This rich tradesman had taken a neighbouring peasant's wife away from him, and he lived with her as both his employee and wife.

Stepan knew the entire business – how the tradesman had done injury to the peasant, how this large, unpleasant woman had left her husband and had now grown fat, and sat sweating over tea, and out of charity treated Stepan to tea as well. There were no passing travellers. They let Stepan spend the night in the kitchen. Matryona cleared everything away and went off to the bedchamber. Stepan lay down on top of the stove but could not sleep, and he kept making the kindling chips that were drying on the stove crackle beneath him. He could not get out of his head the fat belly of the tradesman poking out over the top of the belt of his washed and rewashed, faded cotton shirt. The idea kept coming into his head to slash that belly with a knife and let the fat out. And the woman's too. One moment he would be saying to himself, 'Oh, damn them, I'm leaving tomorrow,' the next he would remember Ivan Mironov and again be thinking of the tradesman's belly and Matryona's white, sweating throat. If he was to kill, then it must be both of them. The second cock crowed. If he was to do it, then it must be now, otherwise it would be getting light. He had noticed a knife and an axe the previous evening. He slid down from the stove, took the axe and the knife and left the kitchen. He had just gone out when the latch on the other side of the door clicked. The tradesman emerged into the doorway. He did it not as he had wanted. He did not get to use the knife, but swung the axe up and cut through the head. The tradesman toppled onto the doorpost and to the floor.

Stepan went into the bedchamber. Matryona leapt up and stood by the bed in nothing but her nightshirt. With that same axe Stepan killed her too.

Then he lit a candle, took the money out of the bureau and left.

16

In the district's main town, at a distance from the other buildings, in his own house there lived an old man, a drunken former civil servant, with his two daughters and his son-in-law. The married daughter drank and led a bad life too, while just the elder one alone, a widow, Maria Semyonovna, a thin and wrinkled woman of fifty, kept them all: she had a pension of 250 roubles. The whole family was fed on this money. And in the house it was just Maria Semyonovna alone that worked. She looked after her weak, drunken old father and her sister's child, and she cooked and washed. And, as is always the way, she also had piled upon her all the things that needed to be done, and she was scolded by all three as well, and, when in a drunken state, her brother-in-law would even beat her. She bore everything in silence and with meekness, and, as is also always the way, the more she had to do, the more she managed to do. She both helped the poor by taking from herself, giving away her own clothing, and helped to look after the sick.

Once, a lame man, a legless rural tailor, was doing some work for Maria Semyonovna. He was altering the old man's coat and covering a sheepskin jacket with heavy cloth for Maria Semyonovna – for wearing to the market in the winter.

The lame tailor was an intelligent and observant man who had seen a lot of different people in his job, and who, in consequence of his lameness, was always sitting, and was therefore disposed to thinking. Having lived with Maria Semyonovna for a week, he could not keep from wondering at her life. One time she came to where he was sewing in the kitchen to wash some towels, and she got into conversation with him about his life, how his brother had been unkind to him and how he had set up on his own.

'I thought things would be better, but it's always the same – dire straits.'

'It's better not to change, but to go on living as you are,' said Maria Semyonovna.

'I wonder at you, Maria Semyonovna, at the way you're always on your own and taking trouble over people here, there and everywhere. Whereas from them, I can see, there's little kindness to be had.'

Maria Semyonovna said nothing.

'I expect books have given you the idea that your reward for it all will be in the next world.'

'We don't know about that,' said Maria Semyonovna, 'but it's just better to live like this.'

'And is that idea in the books?'

'That's in the books as well,' she said, and read him the Sermon on the Mount from the Gospels. The tailor fell into thought. And when accounts had been settled and he went home, he kept on thinking about what he had seen at Maria Semyonovna's and what she had said and read to him.

Pyotr Nikolayich changed towards the common people, and the people changed towards him. Not a year had passed before they had chopped down twenty-seven oak trees and burnt down an uninsured threshing-barn and threshing-floor. Pyotr Nikolayich decided it was impossible to live with those people there.

At that same time, the Liventsovs were looking for a manager for their estates, and the Marshal of the Nobility recommended Pyotr Nikolayich as the best proprietor in the district. The Liventsovs' huge estates provided no income, and the peasants made use of everything. Pyotr Nikolayich undertook to put everything in order and, renting out his own estate, he moved with his wife to a distant province on the Volga.

Pyotr Nikolayich had always loved order and the rule of law, and now still less could he tolerate these savage, coarse people being able to seize, contrary to the law, property that did not belong to them. He was glad of the opportunity to teach them a lesson, and he set about his business very sternly. For the theft of timber he had one peasant sentenced to jail, to another he personally gave a severe beating for not turning off the road and doffing his hat. Regarding the meadows, which were under dispute and considered by the peasants their own, Pyotr Nikolayich announced to the peasants that if they let their livestock loose on them, he would impound it.

The spring came, and the peasants, as they had done in previous years, let their livestock loose on the masters' meadows. Pyotr Nikolayich assembled all his workmen and ordered them to drive the livestock to the masters' farmyard. The peasants were out ploughing, and therefore the workmen, despite the cries of the peasant women, drove the livestock off.

On returning from work, the peasants gathered together and came to the masters' farmyard to demand the livestock. Pyotr Nikolayich went out to them with a gun over his shoulder (he had just returned from a tour of inspection) and announced to them that he would not give the livestock back except upon payment of fifty kopeks per head of cattle and ten kopeks per sheep. The peasants started shouting that the meadows were theirs, that their fathers and their grandfathers alike had owned them, and that there was no such rights for taking away other people's livestock.

'Give the animals back, else it'll be the worse for you,' said one old man, advancing upon Pyotr Nikolayich.

'What'll be worse?' shouted Pyotr Nikolayich, quite pale, going towards the old man.

'Give them back and save any trouble. Parasite.'

'What?' cried Pyotr Nikolayich, and struck the old man in the face.

'You don't dare fight. Take the animals by force, lads.'

The crowd moved forward. Pyotr Nikolayich wanted to leave, but they would not let him. He started to force his way through. The gun went off and killed one of the peasants. A sharp scuffle broke out. Pyotr Nikolayich got crushed. And five minutes later his mutilated body was dragged down into a ravine.

A military court was set up to deal with the murderers, and two were sentenced to hang.

18

In the village the tailor came from, for 1,100 roubles five well-off peasants rented from the landowner 105 *desyatins*[6] of rich arable land, with soil as black as pitch, and let it out to other peasants, to some for eighteen roubles, to others for fifteen. Not a single plot went for less than twelve. So they made a good profit. The businessmen themselves took five *desyatins* each for themselves, and this land came to them for nothing. One of these peasant partners had died, and they proposed to the lame tailor that he join them as a partner.

When the tenants began dividing up the land, the tailor would not have any vodka to drink, and, when talk turned to the question of how much land should be given to whom, the tailor said that everyone should be charged equally, that they should not take anything extra from the tenants, but however much was owing.

'How's that?'

'Well, otherwise we're brutes. I mean, it's all right for the masters, but we're peasants. Things need to be done God's way. That's the law of Christ.'

'And where's this law then?'

'It's in a book, in the Gospels. You come on Sunday, I'll read a bit and we'll have a talk.'

And on the Sunday, not all, but three came to see the tailor, and he started reading to them.

He read five chapters of St Matthew, and they started talking. They all listened, but just Ivan Chuyev alone accepted it. And to such a degree did he accept it that he started living in God's way in everything. And his family started living that way. He refused extra land and took only his share.

And people started going to see the tailor and Ivan, and they started to understand, and they did understand, and they gave up smoking, drinking, cursing with bad words, and they started helping one another. And they stopped going to church, and they took their icons to the priest. And there were seventeen such households. Sixty-five souls in all. And the priest took fright and reported it to the Archbishop. The Archbishop had a think about what was to be done and decided to send the Archimandrite Misail, the former grammar school Divinity teacher, to the village.

19

The Archbishop sat Misail down with him and began talking about the new things that had emerged in his eparchy.

'All because of spiritual weakness and ignorance. You're a learned man. I'm relying on you. Go, summon a gathering, and explain things in front of everyone.'

'If the Archbishop gives me his blessing, I shall try,' said Father Misail. He was glad of this commission. Everything where he could show that he believed pleased him. And when converting others, he was most firm in convincing himself that he did believe.

'Do try, I suffer greatly for my flock,' said the Archbishop, as his plump, white hands unhurriedly took the glass of tea that a lay brother was passing him. 'Why only one jam, bring another,' he addressed the lay brother. 'It hurts me very, very much,' he continued his speech to Misail.

Misail was glad to prove himself. But, as a man less than rich, he asked for some money towards the expenses of the trip and, fearful of the opposition of the vulgar common people, he also asked for an order from the Governor that, in case of need, the local police should provide him with assistance.

The Archbishop arranged everything for him, and Misail, having assembled with the help of his lay brother and cook a hamper of the provisions it was necessary to stock up with

45

when leaving for a remote spot, he set off for his destination. Leaving on this mission, Misail experienced the pleasant feeling of being conscious of the importance of his service and, moreover, of the cessation of any doubts about his faith – rather, on the contrary, he experienced complete certainty about its trueness.

His thoughts were directed not towards the essence of faith – that was recognised to be axiomatic – but towards refuting the objections that were being made with respect to its external forms.

20

The village priest and his wife received Misail with great honour, and the day after his arrival they assembled everyone in the church. Misail went into the pulpit in a new silk cassock with a pectoral cross and his hair combed, the priest took up a position alongside him, as did, at a little distance, the sextons, the choristers, and by the side doors the policemen. Even the sectarians came, in soiled, rough sheepskin coats.

After prayers Misail delivered a sermon, exhorting the defectors to return to the bosom of Mother Church, threatening the torments of Hell and promising absolute forgiveness for those that repented.

The sectarians were silent. When questions began to be put to them, they replied.

To the question why they had defected, they replied that in the Church people did honour to wooden and man-made gods, and that in Holy Writ not only was it not advocated, in the Prophets the contrary was advocated. When Misail asked Chuyev if it was true that they called holy icons boards,

Chuyev replied: 'Just turn any icon you like over, you'll see for yourself.' When they were asked why they did not recognise the clergy, they replied that it said in Holy Writ: 'Freely ye have received, freely give,'[7] but that priests only distributed their grace in exchange for money. At all Misail's attempts to find support in Holy Writ, the tailor and Ivan calmly but firmly objected, pointing to Writ, which they knew thoroughly. Misail grew angry, threatened them with the secular authorities. To this the sectarians said that it was said: 'They have persecuted me, they will also persecute you.'[8]

Nothing came of it, and all would have passed off well enough, but the next day at mass Misail delivered a sermon on the perniciousness of seductors, on how they were deserving of all kinds of retribution, and among the common people leaving the Church talk began to be heard of how it would be worth teaching those godless ones a lesson, so they did not upset people. And that day, at the time when Misail was having a little salmon and white fish with the rural dean and an inspector who had travelled out from town, a scuffle broke out in the village. The Orthodox believers had crowded around Chuyev's cottage and were waiting for them to come out to give them a beating. There were about twenty sectarians, men and women. Misail's sermon and now this gathering of the Orthodox believers and their threatening talk aroused in the sectarians a feeling of anger that there had not been before. The evening had come on, it was time for the women to milk the cows, and the Orthodox believers were still standing waiting, and a fellow who tried to go out was beaten and driven back into the cottage. They discussed what to do, and could not agree.

The tailor said they must have patience and not defend themselves. But Chuyev said that if they had patience like that, they would all be beaten up, and, seizing a poker, he went outside. The Orthodox believers fell upon him.

'Come on then, by the law of Moses,' he cried, and he began hitting the Orthodox believers and knocked one of their eyes out; the rest slipped out of the cottage and returned to their homes.

Chuyev was tried, and for seduction and for blasphemy was sentenced to exile.

And Father Misail was given an award and made an archimandrite.

21

Two years before, from the land of the Don Cossacks, there had come to St Petersburg to study on the women's courses a healthy, good-looking girl of Oriental type, Turchaninova. In St Petersburg this girl met with a student, Tyurin, the son of the Land Captain of Simbirsk, and she came to love him, but this was not the ordinary female love with the desire to become his wife and the mother of his children, but a comradely love, nourished primarily by an identical indignation and hatred not only for the existing regime, but also for the people who were its representatives, and by their consciousness of their intellectual, educational and moral superiority over them.

She was a capable student and she committed lectures to memory and took examinations with ease, and, in addition, she devoured the latest books in huge quantities. And she was certain that her vocation lay not in bearing and bringing up children – she even regarded such a vocation with disgust and contempt – but in destroying the existing regime, which was fettering the finest powers of the people, and in showing people the new path in life, which was shown to her by the latest European writers. Plump, white, rosy, good-looking, with brilliant black eyes and a big black plait, she aroused in men feelings she did not want, and, indeed, was unable to share – so entirely engrossed was she in her activities of agitation and conversation. But she found it pleasant, all the same, that she aroused those feelings, and so, although she did not actually dress up smartly, she did not neglect her appearance. She found it pleasant that she was attractive, yet could demonstrate in practice how she despised what was so valued by other women. In her views on methods for the struggle with the existing order she went further than the majority of her comrades and her friend Tyurin, and accepted that all methods were valid and could be used in the struggle, up to and including murder. But at the same time, this same revolutionary Katya Turchaninova was at heart a very kind and selfless woman who always spontaneously preferred the interests, pleasure and welfare of others to her own interests, pleasure and welfare, and was always truly glad of the opportunity to do something nice for someone – be it a child, an old person or an animal.

Turchaninova spent the summer in a provincial town on the Volga with a girlfriend of hers, a rural schoolteacher. Tyurin was staying in the same district too, with his father. All three saw one another frequently, together with the local doctor; they exchanged books, argued and became exasperated. The Tyurins' estate was adjacent to the estate of the Liventsovs where Pyotr Nikolayich came to work as manager. As soon as Pyotr Nikolayich arrived and took matters of order in hand, the young Tyurin, seeing the independent spirit in the Liventsovs' peasants and their firm intention to stand up for their rights, began to take an interest in them, and would often go to the village and talk to the peasants, developing among them the theory of socialism in general and the nationalisation of the land in particular.

When the murder of Pyotr Nikolayich took place and the court arrived, the provincial town's circle of revolutionaries had good reason for exasperation with the court, and they expressed it boldly. The fact that Tyurin had been going to the village and speaking to the peasants was made clear at the trial. A search was made of Tyurin's rooms, several revolutionary pamphlets were found, and the student was arrested and taken to St Petersburg.

Turchaninova followed after him and went to the prison for a visit, but she was not let in on the usual day, and was admitted only on the day for communal visits, where she and Tyurin saw one another through two sets of bars. This visit further intensified her exasperation. And her exasperation was brought to its absolute limit by her conversation with a handsome young officer of the gendarmerie, who was obviously prepared to be indulgent in the event of her acceptance of his propositions. This brought her to the final degree of indignation and anger towards all figures of authority. She went to the Chief of Police to complain. The Chief of Police told her the same as the gendarme had, that they could do nothing, that there was an instruction from the Minister about it. She submitted a memorandum to the Minister, seeking a meeting; it was refused her. Then she resolved upon a desperate deed and bought a revolver.

22

The Minister was receiving at his usual hour. He passed over three visitors, received a provincial governor, and went up to the black-eyed, pretty young woman in black, standing with a document in her left hand. A tenderly lustful flame lit up in the Minister's eyes at the sight of the pretty petitioner, but, remembering his position, the Minister pulled a serious face.

'What can I do for you?' he said, going up to her.

Without replying, she quickly pulled a hand with a revolver from under her pelerine and, pointing it at the Minister's chest, fired, but missed.

The Minister tried to grab her arm, she swayed back and fired a second time. The Minister turned and ran. She was seized. She was trembling and unable to speak. And suddenly she burst into hysterical laughter. The Minister was not even wounded.

It was Turchaninova. She was put in the house of detention before trial. And the Minister, having received congratulations and condolences from the most high-ranking personages, and even from the sovereign himself, set up a committee of enquiry into the conspiracy, a consequence of which had been this attempt on his life.

There had, of course, been no conspiracy whatsoever, but officers of the secret and the ordinary police forces diligently set about seeking out every strand of the non-existent plot and conscientiously earned their salaries and allowances: getting up early in the morning, in the dark, they carried out search after search, listed documents, books, read diaries, private letters, made extracts from them on beautiful paper in beautiful handwriting, and on many occasions interrogated Turchaninova and organised confrontations with her, wishing to find out from her the names of her accomplices.

The Minister was a kind man at heart and felt very sorry for this healthy, pretty Cossack girl, but he told himself that heavy responsibilities of state lay on him, which he was carrying out, however hard they might be for him. And when a former colleague of his, a chamberlain, an acquaintance of the Tyurins, met him during a ball at court and started to intercede for Tyurin and Turchaninova, the Minister shrugged his shoulders in such a way that the red sash on his white waistcoat wrinkled up, and said, '*Je ne demanderais pas mieux que de lâcher cette pauvre fillette, mais vous savez – le devoir.*'[9]

But Turchaninova meanwhile stayed in the house of detention before trial, and at times she would serenely communicate with her comrades by coded tapping and would read the books she was given, but at other times she would suddenly fall into despair and fury, would beat on the walls, shriek and roar with laughter.

23

Once, Maria Semyonovna got her pension at the government finance offices, and on the way back she met a teacher she knew.

'Well then, Maria Semyonovna, got your government money?' he shouted to her from the other side of the street.

'I have,' replied Maria Semyonovna, 'just enough to stop the gaps.'

'Oh, you've got lots of money, you'll stop the gaps *and* there'll be some left over.'

'Goodbye,' said Maria Semyonovna, and, while looking at the teacher, she bumped right into a tall man with very long arms and a stern face.

But, approaching her house, she was surprised when she again saw this same long-armed man. After seeing her go into the house, he stood still for a moment, turned and went away.

Maria Semyonovna first became terrified, then sad. But when she had entered the house and handed out treats to both the old man and her scrofulous little nephew, Fedya, and given a pat to Trezorka, who was yelping with joy, she began to feel fine again, and, having handed the money over to her father, she set about the work that for her was never-ending.

The man she had bumped into was Stepan.

From the coaching inn, where Stepan had murdered the yardman, he had not gone into town. And it was an amazing thing: not only was the memory of the murder of the yardman not unpleasant for him, but he recalled it several times a day. He found it pleasant to think he could do it so cleanly and skilfully that nobody would find out and prevent him from doing it, either in the future, or to others. Sitting in an inn over tea and vodka, he scrutinised people always from the same angle: how could he murder them. He went to spend the night with a carter from his part of the world. The carter was out. He said he would wait, and sat talking to his missus. Then, when she turned around to the stove, it occurred to him to murder her. He was surprised, shook his head at himself, then took a knife from his boot and, having knocked her down, cut her throat. The children started crying out, he murdered them too and left town without stopping for the night. Outside the town, in the countryside, he went into an inn and had a good sleep there.

The next day he again went into the main town of the district and heard the conversation in the street between Maria Semyonovna and the teacher. Her gaze gave him a fright, but he decided nonetheless to get into her house and take the money she had received. In the night he broke the lock and entered the bedchamber. The first to hear him was the younger, married daughter. She cried out. Stepan immediately knifed her. The son-in-law woke up and grappled with him. He grabbed Stepan by the throat and struggled with him for a long time, but Stepan was stronger. And having done away with the son-in-law, Stepan, agitated and excited by the struggle, went behind the partition. Behind the partition Maria Semyonovna was lying in bed, and, sitting up, she looked at Stepan with frightened, submissive eyes and crossed herself. Her gaze again gave Stepan a fright. He lowered his eyes.

'Where's the money?' he said, without raising his eyes.

She was silent.

'Where's the money?' said Stepan, showing her his knife.

'What are you doing? You can't do this!' she said.

'Looks like I can.'

Stepan went up to her, preparing to grab her by the arms so that she would not prevent him, but she did not raise her arms, did not resist, and only pressed them to her breast and sighed heavily and repeated, 'Oh, this is a great sin. What are you doing? Have pity on yourself. You're damning the souls of others, but your own too, far more… O-oh!' she cried out.

Stepan could endure her voice and gaze no more, and slashed her across the throat with the knife: 'Enough talking with you.' She sank onto the pillows and began wheezing, flooding the pillow with blood. He turned away and set off through the bedchambers, collecting things. Having stolen what he wanted to, Stepan lit a cigarette, sat for a while, cleaned his clothes and left. He thought he would get away with this murder too, like the previous ones, but, before he had reached his night's lodgings, he suddenly felt such tiredness that he could not move a single limb. He lay down in a ditch and lay in it for the rest of the night, the whole day, and the following night.

Part Two

1

While lying in the ditch, Stepan could see continually before him the meek, thin, frightened face of Maria Semyonovna and hear her voice: 'You can't do that,' said her own peculiar, lisping, piteous voice. And again Stepan would go through all he had done to her. And he would become terrified, and close his eyes, and rock his hairy head to shake these thoughts and memories out of it. And for a moment he would be free of the memories, but in their place would come to him first one, then a second black figure, and after the second would follow still more black figures with red eyes, pulling faces and all saying the same thing: 'You did away with her – do away with yourself as well, or else we'll give you no rest.' And he would open his eyes, and again he could see her and hear her voice, and he would start feeling pity for her, and revulsion and terror at himself. And again he would close his eyes, and again – the black figures.

Towards evening on the second day he got up and set off for a tavern. He reached a tavern with some difficulty and started drinking. But however much he drank, drunkenness would not take him. He sat in silence at a table and drank glass after glass. The village constable came to the tavern.

'Who might you be?' the village constable asked him.

'I'm the one that slaughtered them all at Dobrotvorov's yesterday.'

He was bound and, after being held for a day at the police station, sent off to the provincial capital. The chief warder at the prison, recognising in him his former rowdy prisoner and now a great miscreant, received him sternly.

'Mind you don't misbehave here,' croaked the chief warder, knitting his brows and sticking out his lower jaw, 'I only have to notice anything and I'll flog you. You won't escape from me.'

'Why should I run away?' replied Stepan, lowering his eyes, 'I let myself be caught.'

'Well, no talking back to me. And when those in authority are speaking, look them in the eye,' the chief warder cried, and struck him about the jaw with his fist.

At that moment she was appearing before Stepan again, and he could hear her voice. He did not hear what the chief warder was saying to him.

'Wassat?' he asked, coming to his senses when he felt the blow on his face.

'Come on – quick march, there's no call for play-acting.'

The chief warder was expecting rowdiness, arguments with the other prisoners, escape attempts. But there was none of this. Whenever an orderly or the chief warder himself looked in through the spyhole in his door, Stepan was sitting on his straw-filled sack with his head propped up on his hands and continually whispering something to himself. During the investigator's interrogations too he was unlike the other prisoners: he was absent-minded, did not listen to the questions; and when he did understand them, he was so truthful that the investigator, accustomed to fighting the accused with cleverness and cunning, experienced here a sensation like that when, in the darkness, at the end of a staircase, you lift your foot onto a step that is not there. Stepan told of all his murders, knitting his brows and with his eyes fixed on the one spot, in the simplest, most businesslike tone, trying to recall all the details: 'He came out,' said Stepan of his first murder, 'barefooted, stopped in the doorway, and I, like, whacked him once, and he began to croak, so then I set about his missus straight away…' etc. When the procurator was doing his rounds of the jail's cells, Stepan was asked if he had any complaints and if he needed anything. He replied that he did not need anything and that he was not ill-treated. The procurator, after taking a few steps down the stinking corridor, stopped and asked the chief warder, who was accompanying him, how that prisoner was behaving.

'My admiration for him knows no bounds,' replied the chief warder, pleased that Stepan had praised the way he was treated. 'This is his second month here of exemplary behaviour. I'm just afraid he may be planning something. He's a man of courage and inordinate strength.'

2

For the first month of prison Stepan was tormented unceasingly by one and the same thing: he could see the grey wall of his cell, he could hear the sounds of the jail – the hum in the common cell beneath him, the pacing of the sentry in the corridor, the beating of the clock – and at the same time he could see her, with her meek gaze, which had defeated him even on their meeting in the street, and her thin, creased neck that he had slashed, and could hear her touching, piteous, lisping voice: '*You're damning the souls of others and your own. You can't do that!*' Then the voice would die away, and those three would appear – the black ones. And they appeared irrespective of whether his eyes were closed or open. With eyes closed they appeared more distinctly. When Stepan opened his eyes they became confused with the doors, walls, and would gradually disappear, but would then emerge again and come from three directions, making faces and keeping on repeating: 'Do away with yourself, do away with yourself. You can make a noose, you can set yourself alight.' And at this a tremor ran through Stepan, and he began saying all the prayers he knew. 'Mother of God', 'Our Father', and at first this seemed to help. Saying the prayers, he began remembering his life, he remembered his father, his mother, his village. His wolf-dog, his grandfather on the stove, the benches he went sledding on with other children, then he remembered the village girls with their songs, then the horses, how they were stolen and how the horse-thief was caught, how he did for him with a stone. And the first jail came to mind, and how he came out, and he remembered the fat yardman, the carter's wife, the children, and then again he remembered her. And he would get hot, and, slipping the overall off his shoulders, he would leap up from the plank-bed and begin, like a beast in a cage, striding rapidly up and down his short cell, turning quickly by the damp walls, covered in condensation. And again he would say his prayers, but the prayers no longer helped.

On one of the long autumn evenings when the wind whistled and howled in the chimneys, having had his fill of rushing around the cell, he sat down on his bed and felt it was impossible to struggle any more; the black figures had overcome him and he had given in to them. He had already long been looking closely at the air-vent of the stove. If it were to have slender strings or fine strips of canvas wrapped around it, there would be no slipping. But it needed to be arranged cunningly. And he set about doing it, and for two days he prepared canvas strips from the sack on which he slept (when an orderly came in, he covered the bed with his overall). He tied the strips together with knots, making them double ones so they would not break, but would hold his body. While he was preparing all this, he was not in any torment. When all was ready, he made a loop, put it on his neck, climbed onto the bed and hanged himself. But his tongue had only just begun sticking out when the strips broke and he fell. An orderly came in at the noise. The medical orderly was called, and he was taken to hospital. The next day he had completely recovered, and he was taken from the hospital and put no longer into a separate cell, but into the common one.

In the common cell he lived among twenty men as though he were alone: he saw no one, spoke with no one, and was still in the same torment. It was particularly hard for him when everyone was asleep, but he was not, and he could see her, hear her voice as before; then the black figures would appear again with their terrible eyes and taunt him.

Again, as before, he would say prayers, and, as before, they did not help.

One time, when, after a prayer, they again appeared to him, he started praying to her, to her soul, that she would let him go, forgive him. And when, towards morning, he slumped onto his squashed sack, he fell fast asleep, and in his sleep, with her thin, wrinkled, slashed neck, she came to him.

'Well then, will you forgive me?'

She looked at him with her meek gaze and said nothing.

'Will you forgive me?'

And he asked her like that three times. But she said nothing all the same. And he woke up. From then on he began to feel better, and it was as if he had come to and looked around, and for the first time he began to make friends and talk with his cell-mates.

3

In the same cell as Stepan were Vasily, who had again been caught thieving and been sentenced to exile, and Chuyev, who had also been sentenced to deportation. Vasily either sang songs all the time in his fine voice or recounted his adventures to his cell-mates. And Chuyev either worked, sewing something from clothing or linen, or read the Gospels and the Psalter.

To Stepan's question about what he was being exiled for, Chuyev explained to him that he was being exiled for Christ's true faith, because deceitful priests could not bear the spirit of those who lived according to the Gospels and in so doing exposed them. And when Stepan asked Chuyev what the law of the Gospels was, Chuyev explained to him that the law of the Gospels was that you should not pray to man-made gods, but should worship in spirit and in truth. And he told how they had learned this genuine faith from a legless tailor over the question of the division of land.

'Well, and for bad deeds what will happen?' asked Stepan.

'Everything's stated.'

And Chuyev read to him:

'"*When the Son of man shall come in his glory, and all the holy angels with him, then shall he sit upon the throne of his glory: and before him shall be gathered all nations: and he shall separate them one from another, as a shepherd divideth his sheep from his goats: and he shall set the sheep on his right hand, but the goats on the left. Then shall the King say unto them on his right hand, Come, ye blessed of my Father, inherit the kingdom prepared for you from the foundation of the world: for I was an hungred, and ye gave me meat: I was thirsty, and ye gave me drink: I was a stranger, and ye took me in: naked, and ye clothed me: I was sick, and ye visited me: I was in prison, and ye came unto me. Then shall the righteous answer him, saying, Lord, when saw we thee an hungred, and fed thee? or thirsty and gave thee drink? When saw we thee a stranger, and took thee in? or naked, and clothed thee? Or when saw we thee sick, or in prison, and came unto thee? And the King shall answer and say unto them, Verily I say unto you, Inasmuch as ye have done it unto one of the least of these my brethren, ye have done it unto me. Then shall he say also unto them on the left hand, Depart from me, ye cursed, into everlasting fire, prepared for the devil and his angels: for I was an hungred, and ye gave me no meat: I was thirsty, and ye gave me no drink: I was a stranger, and ye took me not in: naked, and ye clothed me not: sick, and in prison, and ye visited me not. Then shall they also answer him, saying, Lord, when saw we thee an hungred, or athirst, or a stranger, or naked, or sick, or in prison, and did not minister unto thee? Then shall he answer them, saying, Verily I say unto you, Inasmuch as ye did it not to one of the least of these, ye did it not to me. And these shall go away into everlasting punishment: but the righteous into life eternal."'* (Matthew 25:31–46)

Vasily, who had taken a seat on the floor opposite Chuyev and listened to the reading, nodded his handsome head approvingly.

'True,' he said decisively, 'depart, like, ye cursed, into everlasting punishment, you fed no one, but stuffed yourselves. That's what they deserve. Come on, let me read a bit,' he added, wanting to show off with his reading.

'Well, and will there be no forgiveness, then?' asked Stepan, who had listened to the reading in silence with his shaggy head bent down.

'Wait, be quiet,' said Chuyev to Vasily, who kept on talking about how the rich people had neither fed the stranger nor visited him in prison. 'Wait, will you,' repeated Chuyev, leafing through the Gospels. Finding what he was looking for, Chuyev smoothed down the pages with his large, strong hand, which had grown pale in jail.

'"*And there were also two other, malefactors, led with him*" – with Christ, that is,' began Chuyev, '"*to be put to death. And when they were come to the place, which is called Calvary, there they crucified him, and the malefactors, one on the right hand, and the other on the left. Then said Jesus, Father, forgive them; for they know not what they do... And the people stood beholding. And the rulers also with them derided him, saying, He saved others; let him save himself, if he be Christ, the chosen of God. And the soldiers also mocked him, coming to him, and offering him vinegar, and saying, If thou be the king of the Jews, save thyself. And a superscription also was written over him in letters of Greek, and Latin, and Hebrew, THIS IS THE KING OF THE JEWS. And one of the malefactors which were hanged railed on him, saying, If thou be Christ, save thyself and us. But the other answering rebuked him, saying, Dost not thou fear God, seeing thou art in the same condemnation? And we indeed justly; for we receive the due reward of our deeds: but this man hath done nothing amiss. And he said unto Jesus, Lord, remember me when thou comest into thy kingdom. And Jesus said unto him, Verily I say unto thee, Today shalt thou be with me in paradise.*"* ' (Luke 23:32–43)

Stepan said nothing and sat deep in thought, as though listening, but he no longer heard anything of what Chuyev read after that.

'So that's what true faith's about,' he thought. 'Only those who've given food and drink to the poor, who've visited prisoners will be saved, and whoever hasn't done that will go to hell. But all the same, the robber only repented on the cross, yet went to paradise even so.' He saw no contradiction here; on the contrary, one thing confirmed the other: the fact that the kind will go to paradise, and the unkind to hell meant that everyone should be kind, and the fact that the robber was forgiven by Christ meant that Christ too was kind. All this was completely new for Stepan; he only wondered why it had been hidden from him until now. And he spent all his free time with Chuyev, asking questions and listening. And by listening, he understood. The broad meaning of all the teaching was revealed to him as being that men are brothers, and they must love and pity one another, and then everyone will be fine. And when he listened, he took everything that confirmed the broad meaning of this teaching to be something forgotten and familiar, and paid no heed to whatever did not confirm it, ascribing this to his failure to understand.

And from this time on, Stepan became a different person.

4

Stepan Pelageyushkin had been humble even before, but of late both the chief warder and the orderlies, and his cell-mates had been struck by the change that had taken place in him. Without any command, out of turn, he would perform all the most onerous tasks, including even the cleaning of the slop-bucket. But, despite this submissiveness of his, his companions respected and feared him, knowing his firmness and great physical strength, especially after an incident with two tramps, who attacked him, but whom he beat off, breaking the arm of one of them. These tramps had set about beating a young, rich prisoner at cards and had taken from him all that he had. Stepan interceded for him and took the money they had won away from them. The tramps started cursing him, then hitting him, yet he overpowered them both. But when the chief warder was enquiring what the quarrel was about, the tramps declared that Pelageyushkin had started hitting them. Stepan made no attempt to vindicate himself and submissively accepted his punishment, which consisted of three days' solitary confinement and transfer to a single cell.

The single cell was hard for him in that it parted him from Chuyev and the Gospels and, besides that, he was afraid that the visions of her and the black figures would return again. But there were no visions. His entire soul was filled with a new, joyous content. He would have been glad of his solitude if he could have read, and if he had had the Gospels. They would have given him the Gospels, but he could not read.

As a boy he had started learning to read and write in the old way: A, B, C, but because of his slow wits he had not gone beyond the alphabet, and then he could not understand syllables at all, and so he had just remained illiterate. But now he decided to learn properly and asked an orderly for the Gospels. The orderly brought them to him and he set about his work. He recognised the letters, but could put nothing together. However hard he tried to understand how words were formed from letters, nothing came of it. He spent sleepless nights, constantly thinking, he did not feel like eating, and in his anguish he had such an attack of lice that he could not comb himself clean of them.

'What, still not got the hang of it?' an orderly once asked him.

'No.'

'Do you know "Our Father", then?'

'I do.'

'Well, read it then. Here it is,' and the orderly showed him 'Our Father' in the Gospels.

Stepan began reading 'Our Father', matching up the familiar sounds with the familiar letters. And suddenly the secret of putting the letters together was revealed to him, and he started to read. This was a great joy. And from then on he started reading, and the meaning that gradually emerged from words that were hard to form gained still greater significance.

Solitude no longer oppressed Stepan now, but gladdened him. He was utterly full of what he was doing and was not pleased when, in order to free cells for newly arrived political prisoners, he was transferred again to the common cell.

5

Now it was no longer Chuyev, but Stepan who often read the Gospels in the cell, and some prisoners sang bawdy songs, while others listened to his reading and his conversations about what he had read. There were two who always listened to him like that in attentive silence: the convict, murderer and executioner, Makhorkin, and Vasily, who had been caught stealing and, while awaiting trial, was in that same jail. Twice during his confinement in prison Makhorkin had performed his duties, both times elsewhere, as people could not be found to carry out the sentences of the judges. The peasants who had killed Pyotr Nikolayich were tried by a military court, and two of them were sentenced to death by hanging.

Makhorkin was summoned to Penza to perform his duties. Previously in these cases he had immediately written – he was quite literate – a document to the provincial governor in which he explained that he had been posted to Penza for the execution of his duties, and thus was requesting the head of the province to assign to him the allowance due for daily subsistence; but now, to the surprise of the prison governor, he announced that he would not go and would be carrying out the duties of an executioner no more.

'What, have you forgotten the lash?' shouted the prison governor.

'Well, if it's to be the lash, then so be it, but there's no law about killing people.'

'What's this, picked it up from Pelageyushkin, have you? There's a jailbird prophet for you, eh? Now just you wait.'

6

Meanwhile Makhin, the schoolboy who had given the lesson in forging a coupon, had graduated from the grammar school and a university course in the Faculty of Law. Thanks to his success with women, with the former lover of an aged Deputy Minister, he was appointed at a very young age to be an investigator. He was a dishonest man, in debt, a seducer of women, a card player, but he was a cunning, bright man with a good memory, and knew how to conduct his affairs well.

He was an investigator in the district where Stepan Pelageyushkin was being tried. During the very first examination Stepan surprised him with his replies, simple, truthful and composed. Makhin unconsciously sensed that this man standing before him in chains and with a shaved head, who had been brought here, was being guarded, and would be led away under lock and key by two soldiers, that this man was utterly free and stood unattainably high above him morally. And for that reason, while examining him, he continually gave himself little bits of encouragement and urged himself on so as not to become embarrassed and muddled. He was struck by the fact that Stepan spoke about his deeds as though of something long past, committed not by him, but by some other person.

'And did you not feel sorry for them?' asked Makhin.

'No. I didn't understand then.'

'Well, and now?'

Stepan smiled sadly.

'Now, if you burnt me on a fire, I wouldn't do it.'

'And why's that?'

'Because I've realised that all men are brothers.'

'What, so I'm your brother too?'

'But of course.'

'How's that, I'm your brother, and I'm condemning you to hard labour?'

'Because you don't understand.'

'And what is it I don't understand?'

'You don't understand, as you're condemning.'

'Well, let's continue. Then where did you go?…'

But what struck Makhin most of all was what he learnt from the chief warder about Pelageyushkin's influence on Makhorkin, who, risking being punished, had refused to perform his duties.

7

At a soirée at the Yeropkins' where there were two young ladies, potential rich brides, both of whom were being courted by Makhin, after the singing of romances, in which the very musical Makhin particularly distinguished himself – he both sang second parts splendidly and played accompaniments – he gave a very accurate and detailed – he had a splendid memory – and completely dispassionate account of the strange criminal who had converted an executioner. Makhin both remembered and was able to communicate everything so well because he was always completely dispassionate towards the people he was dealing with. He did not enter into, did not know how to enter into, the mental state of other people, and it was for this reason he could memorise so well everything that happened to people, what they did and said. But Pelageyushkin had interested him. He had not entered into Stepan's soul, but had involuntarily asked himself the question: what does he have in his soul; and, finding no answer, but sensing that this was something interesting, he gave an account at the soirée of the whole matter: both the perversion of the executioner, and the chief warder's stories of how strangely Pelageyushkin behaved, and how he read the Gospels, and what a powerful influence he had on his companions.

Makhin's account interested everyone, but most of all the younger girl, Liza Yeropkina, an eighteen-year-old who had just left the institute and who had just come to her senses after the ignorance and narrowness of the false conditions in which she had grown up, and, like someone who had come from under water to the surface, was inhaling the fresh air of life. She started questioning Makhin about details and about how and why such a change had taken place in Pelageyushkin, and Makhin told her what he had heard from Stepan about the last murder, and how the meekness, submissiveness and fearlessness before death of the very good woman he had killed last had conquered him, had opened his eyes, and how, later on, the reading of the Gospels had finished the job.

Liza Yeropkina could not get to sleep for a long time that night. For several months a struggle had already been going on inside her between social life, into which her sister had enticed her, and an enthusiasm for Makhin, combined with the desire to reform him. And now the latter took the upper hand. She had heard about the murdered woman before. But now, after that terrible death and Makhin's account, based on what Pelageyushkin had said, she had found out about Maria Semyonovna's story in detail and was struck by all she had learned about her.

Liza conceived a passionate desire to be such a Maria Semyonovna. She was rich, and was afraid that Makhin was courting her for her money. And she decided to break up her estate and give it away, and she told Makhin about it.

Makhin was glad of the opportunity to demonstrate his disinterestedness, and he told Liza it was not for her money that he loved her, and this, as it seemed to him, magnanimous decision of hers touched him personally. A struggle had begun in the meantime between Liza and her mother (the estate had come from her father), who would not allow the estate to be given away. And Makhin helped Liza. And the more he acted in this way, the more he understood the completely different world of spiritual aspirations, until then foreign to him, that he saw in Liza.

8

All had become quiet in the cell. Stepan lay in his place on the plank-bed and was not yet asleep. Vasily went up to him and, tugging at his leg, winked at him to have him get up and come over to him. Stepan slipped off the plank-bed and went up to Vasily.

'Well, brother,' said Vasily, 'will you take the trouble to give me a hand?'

'Give you a hand to do what?'

'I want to escape.'

And Vasily revealed to Stepan that he had everything ready to make his escape.

'Tomorrow I'm going to get them all worked up,' he indicated the men lying down. 'They'll tell on me. They'll transfer me to the upper cells, and there I know what to do. You just loosen up the hasp out of the mortuary.'

'I can do that. But where will you go?'

'I'll just follow my nose. There's quite enough bad people around.'

'It's so, brother, only it's not for us to judge them.'

'Why, am I some sort of killer, or something? I've not killed a single soul, and what's thieving? What's so bad about it? Don't they rob the likes of us?'

'That's their business. They'll answer for it.'

'Why pander to them, though? Say I've robbed a church. Who suffers as a result? I want to arrange things now so I can hit the big money, not just a lousy little shop, and then give it away. Give it away to good people.'

At this point a prisoner got up from his plank-bed and began listening in. Stepan and Vasily parted.

The next day, Vasily did as he had wanted. He started complaining about the bread, that it was damp, incited all the prisoners to call in the chief warder and lodge a complaint. The chief warder came, gave everyone a talking-to and, learning that the instigator of the whole business was Vasily, ordered him to be put in a separate single cell on the upper floor.

This was just what Vasily needed.

9

Vasily knew the upper cell into which he was put. He knew the floor inside it, and as soon as he got there he began dismantling the floor. When it was possible to climb down beneath the floor, he dismantled the ceiling boards and jumped down onto the lower floor, into the mortuary. On that day there was one dead man lying on the table in the mortuary. The sacks for the hay-mattresses were piled here in the mortuary, Vasily knew this, and had been counting on this cell. The hasp in this cell had been pulled out and put back in again. Vasily walked out of the door and went to the latrine that was being built at the end of the corridor. In this latrine was a hole that ran all the way through from the second to the bottom, basement floor. Vasily returned to the mortuary, took the linen sheet off the dead man, who was cold as ice (he touched his arm when taking it off), then took the sacks, knotted them together to make a rope out of them, and took this rope made out of sacks off to the latrine; there he tied the rope to a joist and climbed down it. The rope did not reach the floor. Whether it was short by a little or by a lot he did not know, but there was nothing for it – he hung there, then jumped. He hurt his legs, but he could walk. On the basement floor there were two windows. It was possible to climb through, but there were iron grilles in them. They needed to be ripped out. What with? Vasily began groping around. On the basement floor lay pieces of sawn-off planks. He found one piece with a sharp end and with it began working the bricks that held the grilles loose. He worked for a long time. The cocks were already crowing a second time, and the grille was holding. Finally one side came out. Vasily shoved the plank underneath and put his weight on it; the whole grille worked loose, but a brick fell and made a clatter. The sentries might have heard. Vasily froze. Everything was quiet. He climbed through the window. Climbed out. He needed to escape over the wall. In the corner of the yard was a lean-to. He needed to climb onto this lean-to and from it over the wall. He must take a piece of sawn-off plank with him. You can't climb up there without one. Vasily climbed back. Again he crawled out with the piece of plank and froze, listening for where the sentry was. The sentry, just as he had hoped, was walking up and down the far side of the square of the yard. Vasily went up to the lean-to, put the piece of plank up against it, started climbing up. The piece of plank slipped and fell. Vasily was wearing stockings. He took the stockings off to get a grip with his feet, put the piece of plank back again, leapt up on it, and grabbed hold of the gutter with his hand. 'Don't tear off, old boy, hold me.' He caught at the gutter, and there was his knee on the roof. The sentry was coming, Vasily lay down and froze. The sentry does not see him and moves away again. Vasily leaps up. The iron cracks beneath his feet. Another step, a second, here's the wall. Reaching the wall with his hand is easy. One hand, the other, his whole body is stretching out, and there he is on the wall. If only he doesn't hurt himself jumping down. Vasily turns himself around, hangs by his arms, stretches out, lets go with one hand, the other – 'bless me, Lord!' On the ground. And the ground is soft. His legs are unhurt, and he runs.

In a suburb Malanya unlocks the door, and he climbs in under a warm, patchwork-quilted blanket, imbued with the smell of sweat.

10

Large, pretty, always calm, childless, plump as a dry cow, Pyotr Nikolayich's wife saw from a window how her husband was murdered and dragged off somewhere into the fields. The feeling of horror felt by Natalya Ivanovna (as Pyotr Nikolayich's wife was called) at the sight of this carnage, was, as is always the way, so strong that it stifled all other feelings inside her. And when the entire crowd disappeared behind the orchard fence and the hum of voices fell quiet, and barefooted Malanya, the girl who worked as their servant, ran in, her eyes on stalks, with the news, just as if it were something joyous, that Pyotr Niko-layich had been murdered and thrown into the ravine, out from behind the first feeling of horror there began to emerge another one: a feeling of joy at liberation from the despot with eyes hidden by the dark glasses that had held her in servitude for nineteen years. She herself was horrified at this feeling, she did not admit it to herself, and still less did she express it to anyone. When the mutilated, yellow, hairy body was being washed, dressed and laid in its coffin, she was horrified, she cried and sobbed. When the serious crimes investigator arrived and ques-tioned her as a witness, she saw right there in the investigator's quarters two shackled peasants, identified as the main culprits. One was already old, with a long, fair, wavy beard, and a calm, stern, handsome face, and the other had the stamp of a gypsy, a man not yet old, with shining black eyes and curly, tousled hair. She told what she knew, identified these very men as those who had been the first to seize Pyotr Nikolayich by the arms, and despite the fact that the peasant who looked like a gypsy, his eyes flashing and roaming about beneath his mobile brows, said reproachfully: 'It's a sin, lady! Ah, we're going to die!' – despite that, she did not feel at all sorry for them. On the contrary, during the investigation there arose in her a feeling of enmity, and a desire to take revenge on her husband's murderers.

But when, a month later, the case, which had been handed over to a military court, was concluded, with eight men being sentenced to hard labour and two, the fair-bearded old man and the swarthy gypsy-boy, as he was called, being sentenced to hang, she felt something unpleasant. But this unpleasant doubt, under the influence of the solemnity of the court, soon passed. If the highest authorities deem it necessary, then consequently it must be a good thing.

The execution was to be carried out in the village. And, returning on a Sunday from mass, Malanya, in a new dress·and new shoes, announced to her mistress that they were putting up a gallows, and were expecting an executioner from Moscow by Wednesday, and the families were wailing continually, you could hear it all over the village.

Natalya Ivanovna stayed in the house so as to see neither the gallows, nor the village people, and she wished for just one thing: that what had to be should be finished with quickly. She was thinking only about herself, and not about the condemned men and their families.

11

On the Tuesday, the district police officer, an acquaintance, dropped in on Natalya Ivanovna. Natalya Ivanovna gave him some vodka and pickled mushrooms she had prepared herself. The policeman, having drunk some vodka and had some mushrooms, informed her that the execution would not now be taking place tomorrow.

'What? Why?'

'An amazing story. They couldn't find an executioner. There was one in Moscow, but, my son was telling me, he overdid his reading of the Gospels and says: I can't kill. He's sentenced to hard labour himself for murder, and now all of a sudden – he can't kill even lawfully. He was told he'd be given the lash. Beat me, he says, but I can't do it.'

Natalya Ivanovna suddenly blushed, and her thoughts alone made her break out in a sweat.

'And can't they be pardoned now?'

'How can they be pardoned when they've been sentenced by a court? The Tsar alone can pardon them.'

'But how will the Tsar find out?'

'They have the right to appeal for a pardon.'

'But they're being executed for me, aren't they?' said silly Natalya Ivanovna. 'And I pardon them.'

The policeman laughed.

'Well then, appeal.'

'Can I?'

'Of course you can.'

'But there won't be time now, will there?'

'You can do it by telegram.'

'To the Tsar?'

'Why not, even to the Tsar.'

The news that the executioner had refused, and was prepared to suffer rather than kill, suddenly turned Natalya Ivanovna's soul upside down, and that feeling of compassion and horror that had asked several times to be allowed out, burst through and took hold of her.

'Filipp Vasilyevich, dear, do write the telegram for me. I want to appeal to the Tsar for a pardon.'

The policeman shook his head.

'I just hope we don't get into trouble for this.'

'But I'm the one that's answerable, aren't I? I won't say anything about you.'

'What a kind woman,' thought the policeman, 'what a good woman. If mine were like that, it'd be heaven, and not what it is now.'

And the policeman wrote a telegram to the Tsar: 'To His Imperial Majesty the Sovereign Emperor. Your Imperial Majesty's loyal subject, widow of Collegiate Assessor Pyotr

Nikolayevich Sventitsky, murdered by peasants, falling at Your Imperial Majesty's feet,' (this section of the telegram in particular pleased the policeman composing it) 'begs you to pardon the peasants sentenced to death, so-and-so and so-and-so of such-and-such a province, district, parish, village.'

The telegram was sent by the district police-officer himself, and Natalya Ivanovna's soul was joyful and light. It seemed to her that if she, the widow of the murdered man, forgave and appealed for a pardon, then the Tsar could not fail to pardon them.

12

Liza Yeropkina lived in an unceasing state of rapture. The further she went down the path of the Christian life that had opened up before her, the more certain she was that this was the right path, and the more joyful she became in her soul.

She now had two most immediate aims: the first was to convert Makhin, or rather, as she put it to herself, to return him to himself, to his good, fine nature. She loved him, and in the light of her love the divine nature of his soul, something that is common to all men, was revealed to her; but in this fundamental of life, that is common to all men, she saw his kindness, tenderness and loftiness, which belonged to him alone. Her other aim was to stop being rich. She had wanted to free herself of property in order to test Makhin, but later on she wanted to do it for herself, for her own soul – in accordance with the word of the Gospels. At first she began giving it away, but she was stopped by her father and, still more than by her father, by the host of suppliants that surged forward in person and in writing. Then she decided to turn to a venerable monk, well known for his holy life, so that he would take her money and do with it as he saw fit. Learning of this, her father became angry, and in a heated conversation with her he called her a madwoman, a psychopath, and said he would take measures to protect her, as a madwoman, against herself.

Her father's angry, irritable tone was transmitted to her, and she had not had time to come to her senses before she burst into bad-tempered tears and said a lot of rude things to her father, calling him a despot and even a money-grubber.

She begged her father's pardon, and he said he was not angry, but she could see he was offended and had not forgiven her in his soul. She did not want to tell Makhin about this. Her sister, who was jealous of her attachment to Makhin, distanced herself from her completely. She had no one to whom she could communicate her feeling, no one before whom she could confess.

'You must confess to God,' she told herself, and, since it was Lent, she decided to fast, to tell the confessor everything at confession and to ask his advice about what she should do next.

Not far from town was the monastery in which lived the monk who had become renowned for his life, his homilies and prophesies, and the feats of healing that people ascribed to him.

The monk received a letter from old Yeropkin warning him of the visit of his daughter and about her abnormal, excited condition, and expressing confidence that the monk would set her on the right path – of the golden mean, of a good Christian life, without any violation of existing conditions.

Tired out from seeing visitors, the monk received Liza and began calmly advocating to her moderation, submission to existing conditions and her parents. Liza was silent, flushed and sweated, but when he had finished, with tears in her eyes she began to speak, timidly at first, about how Christ had said: 'Leave thy father and thy mother and follow me',[10] then, becoming more and more animated, she expressed the whole of her notion of the way she understood Christianity. At first the monk smiled faintly and argued back with his usual homilies, but then he fell silent and started sighing, repeating only: 'Oh Lord.'

'Well, all right, come and confess tomorrow,' he said, and blessed her with his wrinkled hand.

The next day he heard her confession and, without continuing the conversation of the day before, he let her go, having briefly refused to take the control of her property upon himself.

The purity, utter devotion to the will of God and the fervour of this girl amazed the monk. He had already long been wanting to renounce the world, but the monastery demanded his work of him. This work brought means to the monastery. And he consented, although he vaguely sensed all the falsity of his position. He was being made into a saint, a miracle-worker, whereas he was a weak man, carried away by success. And the soul of this girl opening itself up to him opened up to him his own soul too. And he saw how far he was from what he wanted to be and to what his heart drew him.

Soon after Liza's visit he locked himself in his cell, and only three weeks later did he emerge into church; he conducted the service, and after the service he preached a sermon in which he censured himself, found the world guilty of sin and called upon it to repent.

He preached sermons every two weeks. And more and more people gathered for these sermons. And his fame as a preacher spread more and more. There was something special, bold, sincere in his sermons. And it was for that reason he had such a powerful effect on people.

13

Meanwhile, Vasily had done everything as he had wanted. With some companions he had got in during the night to the wealthy man Krasnopuzov's. He knew how miserly and depraved he was, and got into his writing-desk and took out thirty thousand in cash. And Vasily did as he had wanted. He even stopped drinking, and gave the money to poor brides. He saw them married, got them out of debt, and he himself disappeared. And the only concern he had was to give the money away well. He gave to the police too. And they did not search for him.

There was joy in his heart. And when he was after all taken, in court he laughed and boasted that the money was lying around wasted at pot-belly's, he did not even know how much he had, whereas I set it in motion, helped good people with it.

And his defence was so cheerful and kind that the jury almost acquitted him. He was sentenced to exile.

He expressed his gratitude and said in advance that he would get away.

14

Sventitskaya's telegram to the Tsar had no effect. The appeals' commission initially decided not even to report to the Tsar about it, but then, when the Sventitsky case came up in conversation over dinner with the sovereign, the director, who was dining with the sovereign, reported the telegram from the wife of the murdered man.

'*C'est très gentil de sa parte,*'[11] said one of the ladies of the Imperial family.

But the Tsar sighed, shrugged his epauletted shoulders and said: 'The law!' and held out his glass, into which a royal footman poured some sparkling Mosel. Everyone pretended to be amazed at the wisdom of the words spoken by the sovereign. And there was no more talk of the telegram. And the two peasants – the old one and the young one – were hanged with the assistance of a Tatar executioner sent for from Kazan, a cruel murderer and perpetrator of bestiality.

His old woman wanted to dress the old man's body in a white shirt, white puttees and new boots, but she was not allowed, and both of them were buried in the same pit outside the boundary of the cemetery.

'Princess Sofya Vladimirovna told me he's a wonderful preacher,' said the sovereign's mother, the old Empress, to her son once. '*Faites le venir. Il peut prêcher à la cathédrale.*'[12]

'No, better here,' said the sovereign, and ordered the monk Isidor to be invited.

All those of high rank were gathered in the palace chapel. A new, extraordinary preacher was an event.

A little old man, grey and thin, came out and looked everyone over: 'In the name of the Father, and of the Son, and of the Holy Ghost,' and began.

At first it was going well, but the further it went, the worse it got. '*Il devenait de plus en plus agressif,*'[13] as the Empress said later on. He lambasted everyone. Spoke of capital punishment. And ascribed the necessity for capital punishment to bad government. Can killing people really be possible in a Christian country?

Everyone exchanged glances, and everyone was interested only in the unseemliness and how unpleasant it was for the sovereign, but nobody showed this. When Isidor had said 'Amen', the Metropolitan approached him and asked him to come and see him.

After a conversation with the Metropolitan and the Chief Procurator, the old man was sent straight back to a monastery, yet not his own, but one in Suzdal, where the Father Superior and commandant was Father Mikhail.

15

Everyone pretended nothing unpleasant had come of Isidor's sermon, and nobody mentioned it. And it seemed to the Tsar that the monk's words had left no trace upon him, but a couple of times in the course of the day he remembered about the execution of the peasants for whose pardon Sventitskaya had appealed by telegram. There was a parade in the afternoon, then an outing to a fête, then a meeting with ministers, then dinner, and the theatre in the evening. As usual, the Tsar fell asleep as soon as he lay his head on the pillow. He was woken in the night by a nightmare: in a field stood some gibbets, and on them swung corpses, and the corpses were sticking their tongues out, and the tongues stretched out further and further. And someone was shouting: 'Your doing, your doing.' The Tsar awoke in a sweat and began to think. For the first time he began to think about the responsibility that lay on him, and all the little old man's words came back to him…

But only from a distance did he see in himself a man, and he could not give himself up to the simple demands of a man because of the demands coming from all sides that were made of the Tsar; and he did not have the strength to admit the demands on the man to be more compelling than the demands on the Tsar.

16

Having served his second term in jail, Prokofy, that lively, proud young dandy, emerged a complete goner. Sober, he sat and did nothing and, no matter how his father cursed him, he ate bread, did no work and, to add to that, strove to swipe things to take to the tavern to get something to drink. He sat, coughed, expectorated and spat. The doctor he went to listened to his chest and shook his head.

'Brother, you need something you haven't got.'

'Of course, that's what you always need.'

'Drink milk, don't smoke.'

'There's a fast on now, and we've got no cow either.'

In spring once he was awake all night, feeling miserable, feeling like a drink. There was nothing to pinch at home. He put on his hat and went out. He went down the street and reached the churchmen's houses. At the sexton's a harrow was standing outside, leant up against the wattle fencing. Prokofy went up, threw the harrow onto his back and set off to take it to Petrovna at the tavern. 'Perhaps she'll let me have a bottle.' He had not had time to move away before the sexton came out onto the porch. It's fully light already, he can see Prokofy taking his harrow.

'Hey, what are you doing?'

Everyone came out, seized Prokofy, put him in the cooler. The Justice of the Peace sentenced him to eleven months in prison.

It was autumn. Prokofy was transferred to the hospital. He was coughing, and his whole chest was bursting. And he could not get warm. Those who were stronger at least did not shiver. But Prokofy shivered both day and night. The chief warder was on an economy drive with firewood and was not heating the hospital until November. Prokofy's body suffered greatly, but his spirit suffered worst of all. He found everything disgusting and he hated everyone: the sexton, and the chief warder for not heating the place, and the orderly, and the man in the bed next to him with a swollen red lip. He hated the new convict who was brought in to them too. This convict was Stepan. He had fallen ill with erysipelas on his head, and he was transferred to the hospital and put next to Prokofy. At first Prokofy hated him, but then he came to like him so much that the only thing he looked forward to was having a talk with him. Only after a conversation with him did the misery in Prokofy's heart abate.

Stepan always told everyone about his last murder and how it had affected him.

'There was no shouting or anything,' he would say, 'but just, here you are, cut me. Have pity not on me, but on yourself.'

'Well, of course, it's a terrible thing to destroy a person; once I took it upon myself to kill a sheep, and I didn't much like that. But I've never killed anyone, and so what have those wicked people destroyed me for? I've not done anyone any harm…'

'So what, everything will go to your credit.'

'Where's that?'

'What do you mean, where? What about God?'

'Somehow he's nowhere to be seen; I'm not a believer, brother – I reckon when you die, you push up the grass. And that's an end to it.'

'How do you reckon that? How many folk have I killed, whereas she, the dear woman, only helped people. So what, do you reckon she and I'll get the same? No, just you wait...'

'So, you reckon you'll die, but your soul will stay?'

'Well of course. That's for sure.'

Dying was hard for Prokofy, he was gasping for breath. But at the final hour it suddenly became easy. He called for Stepan.

'Well, brother, farewell. My death seems to have come. And I used to be afraid, but now it's all right. I just want it to be quick.'

And Prokofy died in the hospital.

17

Meanwhile Yevgeny Mikhailovich's affairs were going worse and worse. The shop was mortgaged. Trade was poor. Another shop had opened in the town, yet the interest payments were being demanded. Money had to be borrowed again at a rate of interest. And it ended with the shop and all the stock being designated for sale. Yevgeny Mikhailovich and his wife rushed around everywhere, but nowhere could they get hold of the 400 roubles that were needed to save the business.

There had been some hope in the merchant Krasnopuzov, whose lover was acquainted with Yevgeny Mikhailovich's wife. But now it was known all over town that Krasnopuzov had had a huge sum of money stolen. People said half a million had been stolen.

'And who was it stole it?' recounted Yevgeny Mikhailovich's wife. 'Vasily, our former yardman. They say he's throwing the money around now, and the police have been bribed.'

'He was a good-for-nothing,' said Yevgeny Mikhailovich. 'How easily he agreed to perjury that time. I just wouldn't have thought it.'

'They say he came into our yard. The cook said it was him. She says he's got fourteen poor brides married.'

'The things they'll think up.'

At that moment some strange elderly man in a woollen jacket came into the shop.

'What can we do for you?'

'A letter for you.'

'From whom?'

'It's written there.'

'So, no reply needed? Won't you wait?'

'I can't.'

And the strange man, handing the envelope over, left in a hurry.

'Odd!'

Yevgeny Mikhailovich tore the thick envelope open and could not believe his eyes: hundred-rouble notes. Four. What's this? And here too a semi-literate letter to Yevgeny Mikhailovich: *'In the Gospels it says do good in return for evil. You done me a lot of evil with the coupon and I done a load of harm to a peasant, but I take pitty on you. Here, have four hundreds and remember your yardman Vasily.'*

'No, that's amazing,' said Yevgeny Mikhailovich, and he said it both to his wife and to himself. And when he remembered it and spoke about it to his wife, tears would come into his eyes and there would be joy in his soul.

In the prison in Suzdal fourteen churchmen were being held, principally for deviation from Orthodoxy; and Isidor was sent there too. Father Mikhail received Isidor in accordance with his documentation and, without talking to him, ordered him to be housed in a separate cell as an important criminal. In the third week of Isidor's stay in the prison, Father Mikhail was doing the rounds of the men being held. On going in to see Isidor, he asked if he needed anything.

'I need much, but I cannot say in front of other people. Give me the opportunity to speak with you in private.'

They glanced at one another and Mikhail realised he had nothing to fear. He ordered Isidor to be brought to his own monastic cell and, when they remained alone, said, 'Well, speak.'

Isidor fell to his knees.

'Brother!' said Isidor, 'What are you doing? Have pity on yourself. There is no villain worse than you, you know, you have profaned all that is holy…'

A month later Mikhail submitted documentation for the release not only of Isidor, but also of seven others, as penitents, and himself applied to retire to a monastery.

19

Ten years passed.

Mitya Smokovnikov had graduated from technical college and was an engineer with a large salary in the gold mines in Siberia. He needed to make a trip around the district. The manager suggested he took the convict Stepan Pelageyushkin with him.

'What do you mean, a convict? Isn't that dangerous?'

'There's no danger with him. He's a holy man. Ask whoever you like.'

'What's he here for, then?'

The manager smiled.

'He murdered seven people, but he's a holy man. I vouch for him myself.'

And so Mitya Smokovnikov took Stepan on, a bald, thin, tanned man, and set off with him.

On the journey Stepan took care of Smokovnikov, just as he looked after everyone where he could, as if he were his own child, and he told him his whole story on the way. And also how, and why, and for what he lived now.

And it is an amazing thing. Mitya Smokovnikov, who until then had lived only for drink, food, cards, wine and women, fell into thought for the first time about life. And those thoughts would not leave him, but wreaked further and further havoc with his soul. He was offered a position where great profit was to be had. He declined, and decided with what he had to buy an estate, marry, and, as best he could, to serve the common people.

20

And so he did. But beforehand he visited his father, with whom his relations were unpleasant because of the new family with which his father had set up home. And now he decided to make friends with his father. And so he did. And his father was surprised, laughed at him, but then of his own accord stopped attacking him, and remembered many, many instances where he had been at fault before him.

NOTES

1. A Russian card game like contract bridge.

2. A Russian measure equivalent to 2.13 metres.

3. A Russian measure approximately equivalent to a kilometre.

4. The People's Houses were centres of popular educational and recreational pursuits in Russian towns and cities.

5. A festival that is celebrated on 8th September.

6. A Russian measure approximately equivalent to a hectare.

7. 'Freely... give' – Matthew 10:8.

8. 'They have persecuted... you' – John 15:20.

9. I could ask for nothing better than to release that poor little girl, but you know – duty (French).

10. This would appear to be a paraphrase of Matthew 19:29: 'And every one that hath forsaken houses, or brethren, or sisters, or father, or mother, or wife, or children, or lands, for my name's sake, shall receive an hundredfold, and shall inherit everlasting life.'

11. That's very kind of her (French).

12. Have him come. He can preach at the cathedral (French).

13. He was becoming more and more aggressive (French).

Leo Tolstoy was born in Yasnaya Polyana in central Russia in 1828. The fourth of five children, Tolstoy was brought up by relatives after the untimely deaths of both his parents. In 1844 he embarked upon the study of oriental languages, then law, at Kazan University, but he never in fact took a degree. He instead returned to Yasnaya Polyana and, in 1851, accompanied by his eldest brother, he moved to the Caucasus where he joined an artillery regiment. It was around this time that he began his literary career, publishing the autobiographical trilogy: *Childhood* (1852), *Boyhood* (1854) and *Youth* (1857).

During the ensuing Crimean War, Tolstoy witnessed the siege of Sebastopol, before travelling widely throughout Europe. These two experiences had a considerable impact on him, and he became firmly convinced that the only way to change the world was to educate it. He thus returned to Yasnaya Polyana and opened a school for peasant children. He married in 1862, and he and his wife (Sofya Andreyevna Behrs, who also acted as his secretary) went on to have thirteen children.

A voracious reader, Tolstoy was determined to understand the world around him. He then sought to explain his philosophical and religious beliefs through his fiction and against a backdrop of world events. *War and Peace* (1865–9), an epic tale set against the background of Napoleon's invasion of Russia, and *Anna Karenina* (1873–7) whose story of a young woman's tragic passion for an officer mirrors a universal quest for the meaning of life, are his two undisputed masterpieces. However, his later, more overtly philosophical works – including *A Confession* (1879–82) and *What I Believe* (1883) – were banned for their supposedly 'dangerous' views, and in

1901 he was excommunicated from the Russian Orthodox Church. Despite this, his writing continued to have considerable influence throughout Russia and beyond, perhaps most notably on India's Mahatma Gandhi.

By this time, Tolstoy had become seriously ill, and in 1910 he died at a remote railway station. His collected works, comprising some ninety volumes, were published in full between 1928 and 1958, and he remains one of the greatest prose writers of all time.

Hugh Aplin studied Russian at the University of East Anglia and Voronezh State University, and worked at the Universities of Leeds and St Andrews before taking up his current post as Head of Russian at Westminster School, London. His previous translations include Anton Chekhov's *The Story of a Nobody* and *Three Years*, Nikolai Gogol's *The Squabble*, Fyodor Dostoevsky's *Poor People* and *The Gambler*, Leo Tolstoy's *Hadji Murat*, Ivan Turgenev's *Faust*, and Mikhail Bulgakov's *The Fatal Eggs*.